Purified

Elizabeth S. Sullivan

Purified

Copyright © 2014 by Elizabeth S. Sullivan

No part of this book may be reproduced or transmitted in any form or by any means without written permission of the author.

This is a work of FICTION.

Names, characters, places and incidents are either a product of the author's imagination or are used fictitiously.

Any resemblance to actual persons living or dead is entirely coincidental.

A SHORT ON TIME BOOK:
Fast-paced and fun novels for readers on the go!

For more information, visit the website:
www.shortontimebooks.com

To Ashley, Kalen, Jim and dearly missed Becky, Sean and Mom.

One

The fact it was drizzling did not dim the useful moonlight, but it did make it harder. The body had been meticulously scrubbed with antibacterial soap; hair shampooed; new white underwear guarded against the old jeans. The plastic gloves and the rain slowed the digging. The skies opened just a bit more, but not enough to wash away progress. Voices from a distance slightly accelerated the final touches. The exact placement of the artifacts was crucial. Finally, success. It was a shallow grave, but it was never meant to be anything other than a beginning.

Two

The Chicago Park teemed with summer life. Amber light washed over the lazy sun worshippers, glazing them in a healthy hue they did not earn. Dogs chased invisible balls and actual Frisbees in the wet grass, almost tripping women pushing baby strollers worth the price of a small car. The low thrum of conversations, an intermittent rebuke handed down to an out-of-line participant was suddenly obliterated by a shrill, inhuman wail. A collective sucking in of breath heralded the series of joy crushing waves everyone knew were coming.

Wave one: a young boy collapsed next to a group of teenage girls. Normally squealers, the girls silently tried to ease the boy out of his fetal position. Reluctantly, onlookers approached, knowing their light reverie was scrolling into some kind of waking nightmare.

Wave two: a chorus of other worldly screeching came from the swings abandoned by fleeing children.

Wave three: a man screeching, "Get the kids away from the goddamned sandbox, get them OUT OF THERE. Call the cops, there's a bloody hand sticking out of the sand." Human sobs were accompanied by police sirens, almost as if they were keeping tempo to the chaos. People fled from the blood and sand.

Wave four: a murdered adolescent girl's mutilated hand reached out of the sand, tripping the boy whose summer dreams would be become nightmares, as would the entire city's.

Three

Beck Oldman stared blankly at the ecstatically happy TV channel shopping host holding a vacuum cleaner hose in a very suggestive manner. Slouched on a cluttered sofa, she nervously tapped a credit card against her outstretched legs that splayed over half empty food containers, books, and beer bottles. Beck's blank stare was not obstructed by the red moccasins on her feet that were propped up on old VHS boxes.

Beck and the TV host shared one thing in common, neither was competent in the domestic arts. Beck appeared as if she didn't know how to clean herself let alone a house evidenced by her stained bathrobe and unruly hair. If Beck wanted to clean her apartment, she could have vacuumed up a storm if only she had opened one of the three boxes labeled VACUUM in bold print. Something awakened her from her stupor. She began to vigorously throw food wrappers and clothes off the sofa, and dug deeply into the cushions. The frenzy was not interrupted by the ringing telephone. An answering machine clicked on, but no cute monologue encouraged people to leave messages. The annoying beep was the only signal the caller had that it was okay to speak. A man's voice boomed from the machine.

"God damnit Beck, answer the phone," he said.

Beck thrust her hands deep down a sofa cave.

"I am not hanging up," insisted Harvey.

Beck triumphantly recovered the TV remote, grabbed the landline phone, and cradled the receiver on her shoulder as she channel surfed.

"What time is it?" she asked sincerely.

"Later than you think. You have your first case. A missing kid from the projects." Beck stopped flipping channels. Her blank face began to register emotion. Her hazel eyes seemed to sink back into their sockets.

"No kids, Harvey."

Harvey's voice took on a somber, yet smooth tone, like a mortician hawking the most expensive casket to the bereaved. "The cops found a murdered girl in a sandbox. You know the kind little kids play in. Her genitals were mutilated and her fingertips were severed. Thirty years of homicide are screaming to me that this kid is the beginning; she is victim one. We have been hired to find a missing girl. You need to get her home before her body parts are found cut up and found in a garbage can."

Beck bolted upright. She held the receiver out in front of her mouth. Just as she began to let him have it, Harvey spoke.

"Be in my office by five. Be on time. Be dressed appropriately, that means you have to peel off those disgusting pajamas and put on actual clothes. I suggest you burn whatever you remove from your body."

"Not working a kid case Harvey, not happening."

"Sure it is Beck. You need this case as much as this kid needs to be found."

There was a loud click, followed by the insistent umm of the dial tone. Beck stared at the receiver, demanding Harvey's return. What she didn't do was call Harvey back.

Beck tossed the receiver across the coffee table, knocking down several empty soda and beer cans. She got up, paced back and forth in front of the TV. She stood in the middle of the spacious living room with a high vaulted ceiling and large windows that would allow for a constant stream of light if the blackout blinds were not shut tightly. Tasteful, sparing decorations marked the room. Finely framed art was carefully placed for viewing. Recessed bookcases stuffed with books and a music entertainment center that boasted a turntable and an impressive library of music. The TV was modest in size but placed prominently in the room. It would be an inviting space if it weren't for the mountains of unopened boxes, clothes, and disorder that reflected Beck's life.

She shuffled her way down a hallway and paused to look at a framed law degree that read Rebekkah Oldman, JD. She went to her large bedroom, a place that offered no respite from the chaos of being Beck. She slumped into the chair next to the computer, began typing, stopped. She went to the mirror by a dresser and stared at her red shaggy hair that stood on end. She touched the half-moon dark circles under her eyes. Small, attractive, mid-forties, her reflection screamed, *hey, need some help here.* When put together, Beck was often mistaken for a much younger woman. There was something youthful about her, maybe her size, maybe the juvenile defiance she often displayed. She was not an easy person.

She walked directly in front of the mirror, nose almost touching the glass. She needed to look this person straight in the eye, this loser who was dangerous to the people who depended on her.

"You stupid bitch, you are not going to fuck up another case, another kid," she shouted. She waited, as if there should be a response.

Shaking her head, she walked away, half angry, half laughing at the show she put on for no one. Then the anger, as it often did, took over.

"God damn you, Harvey, I said no kids, no kids. Shit, where's the phone? Wait 'til I get a hold of you." She held her hands up, turned them over, curled her fingertips. "Why the hell would someone bother to cut off a kid's fingertips, a kid from the projects?" Beck went back to the computer, started typing furiously; she didn't call Harvey to tell him off.

Four

The clouds were heavy, threatening rain, a threat bolstered by distant waves of thunder. The heat of the late afternoon was unbearable, creating a sense of urgency at the crime scene to shut the damn thing down. Sirens of yet another city vehicle heralded its approach. The yellow crime scene tape fluttered loudly as the wind picked up. The morbidly curious craned their necks to see what was in the children's sandbox. Actually they knew a dead black girl was there. They craned their necks to see a murder. Dead is one thing: murder a whole other strata of death, and it was the beginning of a story. What was a black girl doing being found dead here? Now they had a local "who done it" because this park was in the rich, white part of town. If they really wanted to experience murder stories, all they had to do was travel a few blocks to the south side. There murder of young people was so common that if calories were attached everyone would be obese.

Emily Reynolds, a heavily sweating crime scene tech was putting objects into an evidence bag.

"Hey, what have you got there?" She turned around to see who was disturbing her work. "Who are you?"

The young man brushed back his long, black hair. He didn't have a bead of sweat on him which seemed inhuman. He searched the pockets of his jeans and sweatshirt.

Irked, Emily went back to her work.

"Here it is," he said.

Once again she looked at him. He put a detective's badge around his neck, where it lay over Johnny Ramone's face and the title of the Ramones hit, "*I Wanna Be Sedated.*"

"I'm William Blake, before you start, I've heard all the cracks possible about my name." Emily looked perplexed.

"Call me, Will. I just got called. It's my day off. What've we got here?"

Before Will could screw up her scene, Emily went to him. "Adolescent, female, about fourteen years of age, Afr--".

"What's your name?" Will looked at her ID. "Emily, I'm guessing not like Dickinson." She resented his pretty, dry face especially when she had to use her forearm to swipe away sweat that dripped down her neck into her shirt.

"As I was saying, the victim is African American. There was severe genital mutilation. Too early to know if she was raped. Her fingertips were cut off, very Ripper-esque. This is not the kill site. No blood in the sand, and, creepily, she was bathed after death, her hair washed, and her underwear is clean, no, not clean, brand spanking new. There is a crease in it from being packaged, so the…"

"Killer must have bought the underpants before he grabbed her. He knew what size that would fit this particular girl?"

Emily shrugged. "The creepiest part is yet to come."

Emily ran back to the sandbox. Will followed her but she beat him to the grave. She held out a big evidence bag that contained a naked, anatomically correct baby doll and a white, stuffed lamb. Emily pointed to a red line drawn between the legs of the doll.

"That's blood. This whack job placed the doll in her arms, tucked the lamb on her vaginal area, a white, unlit candle next to her head." Will turned to Emily, "So, it looked like someone put her to bed with her doll." Emily nodded. "What fourteen-year-old girl sleeps with a doll?"

Will took the bag, looked at it carefully, maneuvered around Emily to get to the sandbox before she did.

Will spread out his arms in frustration. "Where's the body?"

"Long gone, you're late to the party," she said derisively

Will sucked in his lips, clearly trying to quell something. He walked close to Emily, spoke gently. "Look, what are you, twenty six, seven? How many sites have you worked?"

Emily backed away, also trying to stifle something, the least of which was defensiveness.

"I'm twenty-seven. This is my fifth site. Why?"

"Murder site. Only people on TV or jaded, cynical assholes call a grave, a murder scene a party."

Emily's face was a whirlwind of emotion that finally landed softly.

"Yeah, you're right." Will reached out to shake hands, she complied. "Peace." So what did the coroner's people say?"

"She's been dead at least twelve hours. Her body is almost drained of blood. They stay pretty closed lip on details to techs. No ID, she's a Jane Doe."

Will walked around the sandbox, examined the evidence bags meticulously.

"Candle's never been lit." Emily nodded.

"Did you ever read William Blake's poetry?" Will asked.

"Why, is he a relative?"

"Soul father," Will responded.

"In high school we read some poem about a tiger. I slept through it and what has this got to do with why we're here?"

Will leaned over the sandbox.

Emily jumped in front of him. "Hey, don't touch anything."

Carefully, Will stretched his long frame over the impression where the body had been.

Emily eyed him as she put the evidence bags in a plastic container.

He slyly scooped up some of the sand into a glass vial and tucked it in his pocket.

"I asked about Blake because he wrote about seeing through the mind's eye. Answers, clues, are all right here, right in front of us, like, I dunno, mind prints for us to read. I am trying to see the way he did."

Emily crossed her arms, cocked her head to one side. "Like Blake did. You're trying to see like a dead poet?"

"See like the killer. I want to see through the killer's eyes."

Emily half-laughed, but not out of amusement. "Jesus, you say this shit to homicide detectives?"

Will opened a paper notepad. It was a marked contrast to Emily's state of the art technology. Will wondered if she ever learned how to use a pen or paper. He finally answered her question. "I do keep 'em guessing in the squad room."

Emily looked at him as if he was one of the many corpses she examined; images that had to haunt a young woman's dreams. Her expression jarred Will.

"What?"

"I'm trying to see you with my mind's eye." Will slumped his shoulders with a "give me a break" weariness.

"What I see is okay. Weird, but okay, and I'm betting you're damn good at your job. Can I ask you something?"

"Okay."

"Where did you go to college?"

Will took a weary breath. "Harvard, undergrad, then Columbia, didn't finish grad school."

"What were you studying?"

"Literature," he answered so quietly Emily had to take a moment process to what he said. She pawed the grass with her foot, swiped a drop of sweat from her nose before it plopped on her plastic covered shoes. "And somehow you're a homicide detective."

Will finally exhaled the long breath. "Yeah, somehow."

Emily nodded, thoughtfully. "You got my badge number Blake. If you need help finding the killer's universe in a grain of this sand, call me."

A smile traced his mouth. "I knew you couldn't sleep through Blakes's *Auguries of Innocence*. You dug him, didn't you?"

She smiled. "Nope, sorry. Okay, I'm done here, so you can look--I mean see, without my hovering."

Emily got her things together, turned to say goodbye, but Will was already gone, deep into his mind's eye.

****

Dusk was changing into night. Muffled sounds of thunder could be heard but no sign of rain outside the huge windows. An efficient looking woman in Brooks Brother wear, snapped off her glasses, straightened the artifacts on her desk that already were pin straight, looked around, daring one thing to be out of its place. She sighted the one thing: Beck. Actually the thing she first spied was Beck's leg over the arm of an impeccable leather chair, the frayed end of her jeans fluttering with every nervous twitch of her foot. The clip clop of high heels against the perfectly varnished bamboo floor signaled Beck to get her feet planted on the ground before the tall woman loomed over her.

"May I help you?" Though she obviously tried, she couldn't stop the word *you* from sounding like *youse*. Beck felt trapped in the chair, the woman blocked her. Not good for Beck or the person who cornered her. As soon as Beck got to her feet, the woman, like a cat, faced Beck, rather she looked down at her.

Beck squinted. She stuffed her hands into the bulky, dirty sweatshirt. The logo of the Chicago Bulls and the date 1998 were faded. She put her weight on one leg, cocked her head, and was about to speak but again, the woman beat her to the punch.

"What are you doing here? The agency is closed, has been for over an hour."

Beck looked back toward the entrance, a perfect chance to get away; she never wanted to come, leaving would be a relief, but she had to put the Amazon in her place.

"I have an appointment with Harvey Wilder, one of the owners." Beck put emphasis on the word *owners*.

"Yes, Mr. Wilder, I do know for whom I work, and I know you had an appointment. I booked it. Ms. Oldman, you're late."

"So, what are you saying? Harvey isn't here? He doesn't want to see me? You're giving me a detention? Just what, hey, wait, you're a cop. We worked a case together with Harvey. A woman was raped and murdered. I was the assistant prosecutor on a case six or so years ago. So now you're Harvey's secretary?"

The woman leaned way back, one hand on her hip, lowered her glasses to the bridge of her nose. She peered over them in that annoying way people do, not to see better, but to accentuate a pointed point.

"I am earning three times my former salary as the personal assistant to Harvey Wilder. Yes, I remember you (youse), you're a disbarred assistant DA who's late for an interview for an entry level position for which your services are no longer needed."

Beck took her hands out of her pockets, swung her arm up, and held it in midair. The woman's arrogance switched to a defensive wince, anticipating a hard slap.

"High five."

The woman blinked, shocked. "What?"

"You nailed me, perfectly. High five."

The woman stared at Beck long enough for the arrogance to return in full bloom. She walked to her desk, held up a set of keys, and dangled them in a gesture that signaled Beck to get the hell out of the office.

"No? You don't high five out of principle or you don't high five washed up lawyers? Either way, tell Harvey I meant what I said, no kids. See youse." This made the woman wince on the clear slur against her speech that the short woman in the ugly sweatshirt did perfectly.

Beck reached for the door right at the moment it swung open with a violent velocity that shoved her behind the door.

"So, she just flat out didn't show up," yelled a good-sized man with a shock of thick gray hair. "She's so self-destructive, I've had…"

"IT. With me." Beck moved out from behind the door. "I've been informed that my lowly services are no longer needed. Don't call me, and I won't call you, count on it."

Harvey wheeled around, shocked at the sight of Beck emerging from the back of the door. Shock moved to confusion, then to utter irritation.

"What the hell were you doing back there? You're egregiously late and who the hell told you about your services?"

Beck pointed to the assistant. Harvey followed Beck's arm, his fury landed on the woman.

"Pitt? What the hell did you tell her? Beck, get your ass into my office."

Beck didn't move a muscle.

Harvey looked as if a stroke was imminent. He shoved Beck, and kept on her heels like a herd dog. It wasn't easy.

"Come on, damnit, she's just a secretary." The word secretary happened to coincide as they passed Pitt. Beck shot a look at her that if one were being generous could be interpreted as triumph; if one were accurate the look was a "fuck you. He threw his coat and other items down on a huge desk. The inner office was as lavishly appointed as the reception area, ridiculously expensive furniture, oriental rugs, and massive windows.

Beck stood about one inch from the threshold of the door.

Harvey rummaged through papers until he got a file, tossed it across the desk. It hung on the edge ready to drop.

"You're a mess. Is this your version of getting dressed, and you're late. I hate late."

Beck didn't budge. "I'm not late because I don't work for you which means how I dress is none of your business."

"Sure you do, you work for me," Harvey said in a calm tone. He was in control, he knew it.

Beck ran her hand through her hair that she had slicked down with gel, her version of brushing it. She picked at something on her sweatshirt. Slowly she moved to a chair but didn't sit. She eyed the file that managed to balance on the thin edge.

Harvey sat, he needed to. His sixty six years didn't show, well built, lots of hair, crystal blues that glowed like high beam lights. Handsome in a way that detoured from the mainstream idea of what's attractive. He glowered at Beck but that did not belie the obvious. He liked her in spite of that the fact that she taxed his patience and well being.

"Beck I know…"

"I'm not working with that, that…" She interrupted. She was bored with the Pitt episode; she couldn't be bothered to find a noun she liked.

Harvey was weary; he had only been with Beck for five minutes. "Pitt had my back when we worked homicide. She is ridiculously loyal to me and this firm. She wanted to be a PI, but she fucked up investigations. Little things, but the little things are the thing. We over pay her; she interprets that as position. She has no clout. I will talk with her. Besides, maybe she can help you with, with, well look at you."

Beck looked around the office ignoring his last remark. "You've made a lot of money catching men with their pants down, haven't you, Harvey? That's what I want to do. Set me up to catch some bastard who is cheating on his wife with a girl half his daughter's age."

"I'm employing you not giving you a hobby. We do many kinds of investigations, domestic cheaters, corporate cheaters, and for you, missing people. This firm pulled a lot of tangled strings to get you licensed. We did that because of your expertise prosecuting sex crimes and child abuse cases. Jesus Beck, no one was better at dealing with those scummy bastards than you."

Beck moved to the front of the chair. She fell into it as if her bones had crumbled. "That was a thousand years ago," she said softly.

"Hardly, Beck. I used to skip work to watch you bring those creeps to their knees, begging for a directed verdict rather than deal with you. You were a vision to behold."

"Visions don't get disbarred, Harvey."

"You're not disbarred. You're suspended, let's not have that fight again, Beck."

"Suspended, disbarred, what's the difference? My reputation is wrecked; it deserves to be."

"Here's the difference, disbarred gets you a pass on how you live and dress; suspended, doesn't." Harvey leaned across the desk. "Beck, you were set up, everyone knows it. The Mayor gave you the LeMond case because he knew what it would do to you. He knew you were, um, that you…"

"That I was weak, unstable, had a history, was caught breaking the law? Yeah, lavish me with all of my assets. My assets hurt a kid, no, destroyed a kid."

"Goddammit, stop feeling sorry for yourself and skewing the facts. You said you would work here. You're the one who came up with the pro bono angle. I sold it and you to my partners, so pick up that file and read it, NOW."

Beck took note when Harvey became angry, but listened when he was right. She swiped the file from the desk. Beck's high IQ, and almost photographic memory were her assets and her pitfalls. She would not let anyone get away with the simplest error; her corrections were coarse; she put people off as much as she attracted them. None of this mattered to Harvey. He was always impressed by Beck's skills.

"As you read Jasmine Gordon is thirteen. She lives in low income housing. She's been missing for five days. Her father was told about our new policy. He's exactly the client we had in mind for pro bono cases. This is the perfect first case for you. You know all the people to talk to and you know the area. That kid they found in the park will not be the only dead kid they find. So you need to get your ass out there so Jasmine's home safe."

Beck took the picture of Dennis Rodman from the file. She swung it back and forth. "What is this? This kid doesn't know about the old Bulls which just happens to be my favorite team, and he happens to be my favorite player. You're losing your touch Harvey. It won't work."

Harvey erupted out of his chair, snatched the photo from Beck. "As it happens, smart ass, the kid does love this nut job. If you aren't taking this case, then march your phony do-gooder ass to her father and tell him you could care less if someone tortures and murders his daughter."

Beck stared at Harvey, her hands shook and sweat beaded on her brow. He got her a glass of water. Beck gulped it down. After a few moments, she calmed down. Neither of them acknowledged what just happened. She got up, started for the door.

"Beck, what the hell was that?" Harvey asked genuinely concerned.

"I dunno, happens, maybe I'm experiencing the thrill of early menopause, or just a continuation of, you know. I'm a lame horse, Harve."

"You're a thoroughbred kid, temperamental, high strung, gutsy. Umm, the you know, you haven't gone back to your old ways, have you?"

Beck shook her head.

"But you're spending, using the credit card, right?

Beck didn't answer.

Harvey nodded; he knew.

"You need this job, don't you, and the answer is shit yes. Beck, think about it. You derailed because you didn't save that kid. You can save Jasmine and maybe just save yourself."

Harvey shoved the file under Beck's arm. She started to open the door.

"Menopause. How the hell old are you?"

She flipped him off, which endeared Beck to Harvey even more.

"Oh, Beck, watch my news conference tomorrow. We bagged Richard Safra as a client."

That stopped her. Her expression ranged between horror and shock. "Safra's shit, Harvey. He owns the cops and runs with scum."

"Oh Beck you do care. Don't worry, we can handle the big bad wolf."

"Don't you dare denigrate wolves. Safra's a jackal, and you know it."

"Well the jackal wants us to find his daughter for more money that the US government can print in a day. The public will forgive the scum factor as poor Daddy does all he can to find his kid. By the way, expect a Wilder Employee handbook in hardcopy and E-mail. Highlight the section on appropriate attire. You have lawyer clothes, wear them. A cell phone will be delivered to your place, you're ordered to join this century and to use it."

It was Beck's turn to slam the office door.

***

Will sat bent over his desk at the police station, stared at his notes. He held up the vial of sand taken from the sandbox, dialed the desk phone. He listened, annoyed, as a recorded message played. "Hey, this is Detective Will Blake, homicide. I need a list of newly released inmates from prisons within a fifty mile radius. I want an update on registered child molesters, where they live, if they have…" A loud beep signaled the end of his time to speak.

"Lousy cheap bastards, balancing budgets on dead people." He dialed another number.

"God, you're still there, good man. Did you find any evidence of rape? So nothing? Zero signs of molestation. Yeah, what about semen in her mouth? What did you say? Her teeth were brushed? Jesus. So just to be clear even with the mutilation, you're confident she was not raped and that's because she had no trauma or bruises to…okay, and no ligature marks, yeah, yeah, right of course. Okay, thanks, I'll swing by tomorrow."

Will drummed his fingers on his closed eyes, as if the act would make things become clear. "Look beyond what's in front of you. See beyond the possible and the probable impossibilities," he chanted. He twirled the vial of sand on the desk. "Now how do I see his universe in these?" Will leaned back, turned off the light as he tried to see into a killer's mind and ease his pounding head.

Five

Beck jumped off the bus and landed in a huge muddy puddle. Her attempt to look presentable was assassinated by huge globs of ooze that drooled down her clean T-shirt and sweats. Only her backpack escaped the assault. The summer rain had stopped but the gray sky was heavily overcast. The crap weather did nothing to dampen the throngs of people forging ahead. Humidity makes it hard to breathe and harder to have good hair. Beck left the apartment with hair she liked, but within a moment, the good hair was in the shitter.

Beck stood in the puddle. She raised her arms up to the clouds.

"What's the point of trying? There is no point."

People veered away from the lunatic raging at the heavens. A woman got hung up by the crowd and was stuck next to Beck. Beck looked right at her as she spoke.

"I ask you, in this weather, what is the point of working on this?" Beck pointed to her drooping hair. The woman pointed to her own head that looked like a chrysanthemum.

"I thank you madam for your validation of my sanity."

The woman laughed as she went back into the fray of determined pedestrians. Beck extricated herself from the puddle. Her sneakers squished as she climbed the steps of the police station.

Inside the building Beck took out the stained Bulls sweatshirt from the backpack, put it on and yanked the hood low over her brow. When a couple of policemen entered the building, she turned to look at some pamphlets on a wall rack. After they were gone, she put on sunglasses and moved quickly past the unmanned main desk. She knew every inch of the station; it used to be a second home.

Beck avoided the elevator bank. She climbed several flights of stairs; sweat streamed down her face. Finally she opened a door to a hallway. Beck sucked in a deep breath, screwed up courage but at the last minute avoided speaking to the police woman at the information desk. Instead, she hid behind a pillar. Now what? Then she remembered the cell phone Harvey forced her to activate. He had to give her lessons on how to use it. He was furious with her resistance and had screamed she was a Luddite about a thousand times. Beck already hated the thing, but not right at that moment. She dialed. The phone at the desk rang. Beck watched the police woman say "Missing Persons."

Beck spoke softly, "Yes, I need to speak with Rich Pearce." As if on cue, the very man Beck asked for appeared from an office behind the desk.

The woman indicated that the call was for him. He refused to take it. She rolled her eyes as she lied that he was not available.

Beck just about blew her cover when anger propelled her to move from behind the pillar to look directly at the lying Pearce.

"Oh, yeah, so who is that standing in front of you?"

"Who is, how do you-- where are you?"

"Shit," Beck blurted.

She skulked out from behind the pillar. One look at the small figure in a hoodie and dark glasses prompted Rich and the police woman to draw their weapons.

"Hey, hey, Pearce, it's me."

"Who?"

"Oldman." It finally dawned on Beck what she must look like. She took off the hoodie and glasses. He still didn't recognize her, or more likely, he didn't want to.

"Oldman. I used to be, uh, we worked cases, Rich. Come on, I know you know who I am." Beck walked closer. The closer she got, the more disgust registered in Rich's face.

The guns were put away, but the animosity stayed ready and aimed. The phone rang, which relieved the woman from acknowledging Beck. Pearce and Beck stood face-to-face, like it was high noon in the old West.

"You aren't a prosecutor anymore, what are you doing here?" Rich's voice flowed with contempt and Beck drank it in. She moved toward the main hallway, waved for him to join her, shockingly he did.

"Look Rich, I know on a good day my name is shit around here."

"You sold out the good guys," he shot back.

"They weren't all good…it doesn't matter. I blew it. I know it, but I have a case now. I'm a new, um, I work for Wilder. You know, Harvey, he's put me on a missing girl case. Don't take your anger for me out on this kid."

Rich tied his arms into a knot across his chest. His face was fixed disdain.

She held out the file. Finally Rich yanked it from her hand.

"Hey Rich, how's it going? Excuse me, Ma'am, this will only take a second," interrupted Will.

Beck looked at the clock on the wall for about a second, then insinuated herself in between Rich and Will. "Second's up. Rich, this girl's father...."

"Whoa, whoa, lady. I'm here on official business, a homicide case." It may have been gentle, but a push is a push and Will pushed Beck ever so slightly out of his way.

For the first time Rich did not look like he was sucking a lemon. On the contrary he enjoyed their vying for his attention and any discomfort to Beck was a comfort to Rich. Beck knew she was at a disadvantage. The teenage cop was winning their tug of war just by the fact he was not her.

"Hey, watch who you are shoving, and another thing, enough of the lady and ma'am crap. What is that? And even though you didn't ask, here's a tip. This is the Missing Persons department. Where people assume the persons are still living. You need the homicide division, that's where people know people are dead. Don't worry, rookies often make that mistake." Beck gestured Will's dismissal as she reclaimed Rich's attention.

Will was half amused, half irritated when she turned her back on him. He tapped Beck on her shoulder. She turned to find his shield about an inch from her face.

"Wow, look at that. Was that in a cereal box?" Rich had to bite his lip. He couldn't give her any points.

Will stood back, surveyed Beck's dirty clothes, dirty hair, and tried to guess her age. She looked young and then not so young. "So where's your badge?"

Beck went from fight to flight, instantly. "I'm private, you know, a private investigator."

"Do you have a card?" he asked in a superior tone.

Beck shook her head.

Then it hit him. "You're a rookie? Interesting turn of events, I like to support middle aged people forging a new career in the second half of their lives. PI, that's tough but at least you have AARP in case you get hurt or anything."

Rich let out a half snort, half laugh. "Bull's eye, Blake." He slapped Will on the back as he walked to a water fountain.

Beck threw the hoodie over her head; low to her brow. She hid inside the fleece cave.

Will watched her, she reminded him of a turtle in retreat. He regretted his remarks. She hadn't offended him, on the contrary, he enjoyed the banter of the unusual and attractive woman. He wanted to reach out to her but he sensed she would interpret anything now as an attack. Why was she so familiar? Then it hit him like a volt of electricity.

"You're Rebekkah Oldman." His cell rang. "I got to answer this. You get what you need from Rich. If I can help with your case, call me, before we have to meet up at homicide. By the way, Oldman, I think you got screwed last year." Will handed Beck a card before he left.

Beck watched him until she was sure he was gone. There was something about him, maybe she could trust him. Moments later Rich returned very unhappy to see Beck waiting for him, alone.

***

That evening the drugstore was not crowded. There was only one register with an actual human cashier stuffed way in the back. Customers were forced to use self-checkout stands where even a few people created a long line. On the average it took three shots to get the mandatory plastic card accepted and most people were slow at bagging purchases. The so-called convenience was damned inconvenient. In theory Beck hated stores that used machines instead of people. In practice, there were times they were perfect for her particular needs.

Beck walked down the aisles, occasionally picking up an item that she examined, artfully. An act that she had perfected over the years. She knew how to survey shoppers and clerks, if there were clerks, and appear to be engrossed in shopping. She moved swiftly down the cosmetics aisles with all the false claims of restored youth. In her dirty clothes and mangled hair, Beck looked suspect. She planted herself in household goods, by the rat traps. There she feigned the actions of a customer weighing options, one set of traps in each hand. The conflicted expression was not about the quality of the traps, it was the reflection of the horrible compulsion and war that raged inside her. She carefully set one trap down on the lower shelf, as she did the other trap was stuffed under her sweatshirt. Carefully she walked toward the exit. As Beck got closer to the door, she breathed heavily, little beads of sweat started to pop. She lingered at the display of impulse items, pulled a bag of candy from a hook knocking several bags of snacks to the floor. She looked around. No one cared, or noticed. It was easy, too easy. She exited. On the floor next to the bag of candy, lay the trap Beck almost gave into.

***

That time before total dark and the last gasps of dusk gave little warning to the crater sized holes in the road. There were no working lights to avoid them. Darkness is bad, potholes are bad, but those hardships are easy in contrast to the other degradations this part of the city dishes out. All cities have these sections.

There are many name of these areas. Public housing, low income housing, government housing, and the projects. Projects, that's the most accurate name. The definition of project when it is used as noun means an undertaking, a scheme, an expensive task requiring a concerted effort. As a verb it means to thrust out, cast away, send out to space. The people who live in the projects have been cast out, and there is a concerted effort to ignore their plight. Those in power don't care that gun violence, drugs, and health in the projects have some of the same horrible statistics of war zones. No one cares outside of the projects unless the violence leaks out into mainstream of the things.

    The black sedan avoided bottoming out, deftly. The tired basketball court showed its weariness by the ripped nets and the broken asphalt; yet the girls played vigorously under the unreliable lights. They went out often, leaving the girls in a valley of darkness. It would last for seconds or minutes. Sometimes the darkness lasted so long, a girl would leave out of frustration and no one would notice until they started to play again. A lot of things happened on that court because of the fickle lights. The nondescript sedan parked across the street. Patience that had been taught as a virtue became a valued weapon for the person behind the steering wheel.

Six

Ms. Pitt, perfectly starched, was in her element. The hand-selected members of the Press were in the exact formation she demanded. They had assembled as ordered by one thirty. A podium was set up outside the doors of Harvey's office. The small cadre of reporters quietly worked on their various electronic devices. One TV news crew stood to the side, watched Pitt for the signal. The anointed few were there for the biggest story of the week. A press conference called by Richard Safra. The first one since his daughter was reported missing. A curt nod from Pitt triggered perfect harmony of the opened doors being flooded by harsh white lights. Harvey stood at the threshold. His thousand dollar suit did not strip away the patina of three decades in homicide. There was no hiding the years of gulping gallons of scorched coffee while he examined the remains of what was once a human being. Harvey always told rookies if they didn't plan to live a life immersed in perversion, they should become salesmen instead. Homicide was Dante's Hell. The clicks of cameras went on for several moments as he surveyed which members of the press were present. He took a mental note of who stood where.

After he catalogued the players, Harvey stepped aside for Richard Safra, a man whose reputation created fear and awe. Tall, blond, a chiseled face that only slightly softened after sixty-five years of living. He was not handsome. Safra's face was too perfect, like a wax figure, smooth, and devoid of humanity. It was a face people had to stare at, the way people do a car wreck, or when a snake slithers away. It was hard to tell if his eyes had pigment, but on close inspection, if one dared, the hint of blue was there. It was disconcerting when he stared at someone, especially if that someone displeased him. Everyone had to look away from his cold gaze. Once he entered the room, no one remembered that they were at Harvey's office, or even who he was. If someone could literally take the oxygen out of the room, it would be Richard Safra.

It was a dicey game to be a reporter because no one wanted to exact his anger. There was a sense of imminent chaos. The press had waited far too long to question him about his missing daughter. How could they build on that issue and finally get to ask about his businesses and the political ties to those who were in power legitimately and those who simply seized it. Pitt realized her control was no longer in play. She drifted to a back corner.

Safra's smoothness was accentuated by the lighting; a poster for Botox ads. The microphone needed to be adjusted, but Safra did not touch it.

A young man of Middle Eastern descent, impeccably dressed in a suit and tie, fixed it very quickly. He never took his eyes off of Safra. As quickly as he appeared, he receded to the back of the room. Harvey clearly had never seen this man before, he seemed disconcerted by his presence.

Safra finally began to speak, his voice had the timber and cadence that radio announcers covet. He could sell death to the living. "As you know I have suffered a loss. It has been five weeks since she has been missing. There have been no ransom demands, messages, threats, nothing. It as if she never existed. Of course that means there are no leads and no progress. People have said to me that I have to accept that the situation is, shall we say, dire. I refuse to accept that assessment. Therefore, I have decided the police need help. I have hired the Wilder Agency, headed by Harvey Wilder to conduct an investigation. Mr. Wilder's experience will be an important adjunct to the police department's work."

The flashing lights created a strobe effect. Harvey moved to the microphones on Safra' command. He waited for order and quiet in the room. "Thank you, Mr. Safra. We are honored that you trust our agency to help find your beloved daughter, Olivia Safra."

From the podium Harvey held up a blown-up picture of a young, biracial girl. Her face was blank, devoid of emotion, like her father's, but that's where the resemblance stopped. She had dark, vibrant eyes, thick black hair. Pitt handed out smaller copies to the reporters.

"Unfortunately we do not have a more recent picture of Olivia. In this picture she is fifteen. Olivia is twenty-two and a premed student. The last time Mr. Safra spoke to his daughter was in May, but these are old facts. We will hand out a summary sheet to you as you leave. What is new is that we are offering a reward for any information that gives us a lead to the whereabouts of Olivia Safra or to her captor, five hundred thousand dollars cash."

Pandemonium. The reporters fired so many questions that the result was nothing more than a tangle of incoherence.

No reaction or attempt to put things in order came from the podium or Pitt, who bit her nails in a dark corner. Harvey enjoyed being at the center of the storm.

Finally a voice cut above the herd. "Mr. Safra, why don't you have recent photographs of your only child?"

Silence, the deafening kind. Safra surveyed the room to find the owner of the question. He found him when the Middle Eastern man nodded to the reporter who stood next to him. The reporter was about to ask another question but stopped when the Middle Eastern man spoke to him.

"Repeat the question and show yourself," demanded Safra. No response.

The door to the reception area closed after the reporter exited.

Harvey motioned to Safra to return to his office.

Safra did not condescend to Harvey's wish. Instead he leaned into the microphone.

"Mr. Wilder neglected to mention that Rebekkah Oldman will be the lead detective on the case."

Shock surged through the room. Finally, one person found his voice. "Do you mean Rebekkah Oldman the ADA who was fired after losing the LeMond child abuse case? Who suffered a mental breakdown? She is, or she was a lawyer. Why is she the lead investigator? For that matter, Mr. Wilder, why did you hire her?" Questions floated in the air like a balloons of shit ready to be popped.

Safra's expression was no longer inscrutable; it had the unmistakable look of a predator.

Harvey's arrogance was replaced by confusion. He wanted the answers more than the reporters. Safra ever so lightly moved his hand, Harvey obeyed the order and moved to the microphones but had no idea what to say. He had no idea what was safe to say because Safra had usurped his role as CEO his own company.

Who the hell was Safra to put Beck on the case? Of course, that was just it, Harvey knew exactly who, more importantly what Safra was.

The reporters finally got over their shock and resumed chaos.

Safra again gave a slight indication of what to do. Harvey turned his back to the Press, waited for Safra to enter his office first. A little voice told Harvey to show that deference, it also made him wonder if Beck wasn't right about working for Richard Safra. He swiped something from his sleeve, maybe a trace amount of scum.

****

Janice looked like a fish gulping for air. She stared at the TV on the wall across from the worn oak bar. Someone yelled about the game. In an instant the screen flipped from showing an empty bank of microphones in Harvey's office to fans in a stadium. Janice slowly turned to Beck with a "what the hell was that" look. Beck looked at the screen as a player swung his bat long after the ball landed into the catcher's mitt. A young woman with menus approached them. "Janice, your table is ready."

Janice gathered up her trendy handbag and gigantic sunglasses. She dismounted from the high bar stool with grace, landed a perfect ten on very tall heels. She followed the young woman until she realized that she was the only one doing so. Beck was still at the bar.

"Beck, Beck, our table is ready."

The bartender tapped Beck's hand. She responded like someone awakened from a deep sleep, thoroughly confused by the empty bar stool next to her. She finally figured out that the annoyed woman staring at her was in fact her missing friend. Beck mouthed the words: "What the fuck," as she pointed to the TV. Janice had been an ER nurse so she knew when someone was borderline crashing. She went back to get Beck's purse. Janice was thrilled it wasn't a backpack. She took Beck by her elbow and guided her to the table where the young woman waited. After they received the menus, Janice waved the waitress over and ordered two emergency martinis.

As soon as the drinks were set down, Beck drained her glass. She signaled for another round before Janice even picked up her glass.

"Why didn't you tell me?" Janice asked after she finally got a drink.

"Didn't tell you what?" The second round arrived. In between gulps Beck munched on the green olives, her jaw worked overtime on the gin-soaked treats.

Janice was bugged. "Come on. What's going on? You're out in public, something's up."

Beck played with the masticated remains of pimento between her front teeth, spit them out along with the words, "Fucking Safra, fucking Harvey."

The waitress approached, ready to take their order. Beck spoke very slowly, succinctly as if her sequenced words were the only thing keeping her sane.

"We'll let you know when we're ready, in the meantime, please keep the drinks coming," she said carefully.

Janice was in her own struggle to sound calm, but her words exploded.

"Why the hell would Safra want you to find his daughter?" Just about everyone in the dining room stopped. After they gave Janice the obligatory scoff for poor manners, they turned their attention to the disgraced, former Assistant District Attorney, Oldman.

It was a crude way of putting it, but Janice had a damn good question. Beck noticed that the people seemed to be waiting for an answer.

Beck swooped up her martini, stood up and addressed the diners. "Why the hell did Richard Safra just manipulate me into working for him? Hell, I wouldn't hire me, my being so screwed up and all. Never fear, folks, it's not like I had the balls to think for a single minute that I deserved a break, a second chance, a nod of confidence. Be assured that I am as humiliated and ruined as the day I left my office. Be assured that my public damning has not ended." Beck held up her drink, toasted the air, slugged down the last little bit of alcohol.

Janice lowered her head. Beck patted her hand. "Don't worry, I am used to the public's disdain. There is an ugly something that Safra has up his sleeve that forced Harvey to put me on the case. Did you see him? He was shocked. Safra blindsided him. It was a good question, Janice, just next time you want to ask me something, maybe you could lower the decibels by a thousand?"

Janice laughed but the last thing she wanted to do was draw more negative attention on her weary friend. "How are you doing? Are you still seeing…"

"A shrink? Yeah, off and on, just enough to keep myself well supplied in pharmaceuticals. I have enough drugs to supply the

Army. Why?" Beck asked in a voice that revealed anger and vulnerability.

"I'm just checking on my friend, Beck, that's all."

Beck's torso twisted in the plush chair. Janice had to switch the mood. "Your hair looks great, longer," she said in a genuine tone.

"Yeah, neglect has its rewards."

"You'll get back to your old self now that you're working."

The martinis arrived. Janice drank first; she needed it.

"I called you to tell you that Harvey hired me to find a missing girl. I accepted the job obviously not anticipating Safra. Shit, now I am torn."

"You were hired to find the dead girl from the sandbox?" Janice gasped.

"Jesus, no. I haven't screwed up already. That girl is not Jasmine, the girl I need to find. Of course no one knows that she's missing, or anything about the girl in the sandbox because they're poor kids from the projects. Can you imagine if they were white girls?" Beck pointed back to the TV screen. "If either of them had a Daddy named Safra, the police force and media universe would be all over it and you would know who their kindergarten teachers were." Beck's voice was strong, no quiver or vacillation.

Janice leaned across the table. "Doesn't sound like you're torn about finding Jasmine, but as to Safra, I'd rather kiss a Black Mamba than shake his hand. The only reason he's not in prison is because he owns everything and everybody."

Beck smiled, "It's because they can't catch him. I used to hear things when I was working in City Hall. There was a lot of hatred for him by the cops and politicians, but no one could touch him, even the Feds. He is a mastermind."

Janice looked around for the waitress. "The cops have got to be shitting their pants that they can't find his daughter. And how about that reporter, challenging him? What do you bet he wakes up with a horse's head at the foot of his bed?"

Beck shook her head. "I don't take sucker bets. I'm not going to work for him which makes Safra look like a fool and that's not good for Harvey. That reward, no way Harvey was behind that. Money only brings out the crazies. Safra just put the investigation into the toilet. Safra said one big "fuck you" to the men in blue, then he added the cherry of me on the top of their shit sundae."

"Beck, it's great that you're working and I know you'll be able to handle what the media and cops dish out. What concerns me Rebekkah, is you working a case that involves a young girl."

Beck looked away from Janice because she was right. She hated to let her know she was right for lots of reasons, but this time because Beck knew Janice should be worried about her.

"Rebekkah, you are worried. Harvey convinced me when he said that finding Jasmine could help me. I need to make amends for what happened; it's no joke what I said. Maybe if I find Jasmine, I can find a little piece of myself. Okay? I have an expense account, this lunch is on Harvey so let's burn up his credit card."

Beck waved over the waitress; Janice sucked out the last dribble of martini.

***

The black sedan pulled into the rest stop. It was another busy afternoon. People stretched from long road trips, let their dogs relieve themselves, ate soggy sandwiches that were packed too many hours ago. The bathroom, especially the women's, was the main destination spot. So no one noticed that the person in the baseball cap. After all everyone had some version of that cap; no one noticed that person wiping down a basketball with sanitary wipes; or noticed that the cleaned ball was buried in the trash. There is an understanding and unspoken rule about rest stops. Everyone knows that there are strange people at rest stops, serious, carnie worker strange. The unspoken rule of the road warrior when taking time out at a rest stop is to live and let live. The black sedan pulled out as unnoticed as it pulled in, leaving behind the object that had brought so much hope and joy, buried in melting ice and rotting sandwiches.

***

Rolling thunder can be romantic or mysterious in a well-decorated apartment that has a great view of the city. In the graffiti covered, dark hallways of the projects it sounded like gunshot, or the backfire of a car, or the bass on a car stereo. It was just another addition of the never-ending sound that radiated throughout every nook and cranny of the inhabitants' lives twenty-four hours a day. Constant noise is torture. Governments literally torture prisoners with endless noise.

Beck negotiated her way down the dark halls confidently. She had been to these projects when she was a prosecutor. It wasn't just interviewing a witness to a heinous crime that was committed in the building, or talking to the mother of the victim in the woman's blighted apartment that made feel Beck feel guilty about her fine home. It was the fact that she never felt like she belonged in anything better than the projects. Beck grew up hard; she knew how to negotiate the tough landscape of poverty. For Beck, easy was difficult, alien. She had to resist her impulses to sink into the familiar feelings of want and unworthiness. Her apartment never felt like it was her home. It was merely evidence that she had escaped material misery.

Beck looked at the file one more time before she knocked on the door. She was dressed the way Harvey demanded in a text message. She hated the nagging phone. He sent her clothes to wear. The severe black jacket's sleeves were too short. The white shirt was overly starched. She was sure Pitt did that. Finally the black, straight legged trousers just hit the top of her ankle. Beck's hair was smooth and glossy. Her makeup brightened her face.

When the door opened, a shadow was cast over Beck. The tall African American man wasn't thrilled to see the figure who interrupted his day filled with fear and anger.

"I don't want any of your Jehovah's Witness messed up shit. How many times do I have to tell you people? I want to burn in hell. Now get out and stay out for eternity."

Beck looked behind her, down the hallway, each way, then back to the man railing at her.

"What makes you think I'm a Jehovah--?"

"You're wearing the uniform, aren't ya?"

The man glared at her. She didn't need him to answer. "Goddamn that Harvey. I told him I looked like a nun, not to mention it is hotter than hell." Now the man scowled at the irritated woman slightly surprised. "What do you want?"

Beck didn't hear him. She was thinking how much she wanted to punch Harvey.

"Lady, what- do- you-WANT?"

Beck rankled at the word lady. "I want to speak to Miles Gordon. I work for that jerk, Harvey Wilder. Are you Mr. Gordon?" She asked, tersely. She searched the pockets of her tight black trousers, pulled out a slightly bent card. She gave it to Miles. After he read it he was more annoyed.

"About damn time." He entered the apartment, left the door open. Beck waited to be invited in.

"Are you coming, close the door," bellowed Miles.

Beck swore under her breath as she entered. She left the door wide open. She moved out of a small dark foyer into a clean, compact apartment. A worn sofa was bookended by small tables that were burdened by the many framed pictures chronicling the life of Jasmine Gordon. Her smiling face as a baby to the strong girl of fourteen, and every stage in between was on display. Beck stopped at one picture that showed Jasmine in a Dennis Rodman jersey, number 91. She turned to Miles, her unspoken question was answered by a nod. Beck picked up the picture, touched it lightly. She put it down in its exact spot.

"How does a kid today know about Rodman?" she queried.

"She gets taught by her daddy. I told her if a guy like that can make it, tough it out when everyone is against you, even your own upbringing is against you, then Jasmine sure as hell could get whatever she had a mind to."

Beck nodded. "Even with all of the tats and bad boy behavior, he's like a kid, naïve. He really believes his going to North Korea could fix things. Just hangout, say you're sorry and all transgressions go away. Kid thinking. Anyway, he was a damn good rebounder."

Miles watched her. "So how are you going to find Jasmine when you're too busy finding the rich man's kid? Maybe Jasmine is a warm up for King Safra's daughter."

Beck wanted to sit, but hadn't been asked. She shifted from one foot to the other, more from irritation than fatigue. "You mean because of that circus on TV? You do know not to believe pretty much anything on TV, the Internet, nothing on social media, right?"

"So, everyone's a liar?" Miles asked.

"Everyone but me." He was not amused and neither was Beck. "Look, Mr. Gordon, I can assure you that finding your daughter is my only concern. Jasmine's disappearance is the only case I am working."

"Don't bullshit me, lady. The cops haven't lifted a finger. Hell, haven't heard nothing about them trying to find the killer of the dead girl from the park. Now if that girl was white, all of us on this side of town would have a visit from the cops. You know, questioning our whereabouts and such. So stop the BS."

Beck tried to be deferential as Harvey lectured her to be, and she tried to check the swearing, which always got her written up, but her old self was always lurking about.

"You know I have been told that bullshit is an art I need to cultivate because I am too direct. I tell it like I see it. So here is what I see. First, I am not a damn cop, okay? What they do or don't do, has nothing to do with me, so get off of my back about it. Drop a note in their suggestion box. Second, you're damn lucky the Wilder Agency picked you for their first pro bono case.

Which by the way, was my idea, the pro bono. I don't give a shit about Safra. Did you see me on TV, at the conference? No, no, you didn't. You see me now though, don't you? Here, here, not looking for Olivia. So, why don't you finally ask me to sit my ass down so we can get to work or I can go home, change out of these clothes which got me fingered by you as a religious zealot?"

Miles's mouth gaped open, he pointed for her to sit her ass on the sagging sofa. Beck sank more than sat on the worn out cushion. Miles eased himself into a chair across from her. His skepticism was a third occupant in the room. Beck actually admired him for not buying Harvey's line of crap but didn't want him to know that now.

"So, Mr. Gordon, from what I read from the preliminary file and what could be gotten from the police, there is very little here about Jasmine's mother."

"Yeah, and?"

"And, tell me about her."

Miles looked as if he sat on the edge of a razor, a slight slip would yield disaster. Beck got out her notepad and pen. No electronics. She wrote swiftly, as if lightning were pushing her pen.

"Diana was a pro."

"A pro at what?" She only looked up because she thought she could hear Miles' smirk.

"Are you for real? What is Wilder passing off here?"

Beck rolled her eyes with an 'I'm stupid' expression. "Yeah, okay, I just didn't want to make an assumption because that would have pissed you off if I said of course her mother was a whore."

Miles could not believe her. Who talks like that, he thought. "Actually, I didn't get it at first. I was an asshole thinking that she was taking night classes, I bought it. We'd been married a few months, then I got a call to come bail her out of jail. I was pissed, shocked, everything, but what I was mostly was scared shitless about AIDS. I wanted out, done with her." Sadness crept in around the edges of Miles' undeniable fear. Beck knew that this man never had a moment of peace since Jasmine went missing. She knew there wasn't a second where he did not think his daughter may be murdered.

"But?" Beck's pen was poised to write the answer. She didn't look up to see why he had stopped speaking.

"But she told me that she was knocked up, her words. No way do I care because I think can't be my kid. She's a whore, but the truth was I wanted to be a father. I wanted a child to raise, not just proof that I wasn't shooting blanks. I waited and there was no denying," he pointed to the pictures of Jasmine, his clone, "that Jasmine was mine."

Beck glanced at Jasmine's pictures. "Does Dianna see Jasmine?"

"Di hit the streets right after Jas was born. She won't give up the money, and I think she gets a sick thrill from the danger. I had to fight her not to trick when she was pregnant, guess men pay a lot for sick shit like that. Di is a lot of things but she loves her kid and Jas loves her back. Jas doesn't know what her mama does because Di doesn't want to her to know anything about that vile life, so don't you even think for a minute she'd hurt her. She wouldn't take her from me because it would kill Jas..." Miles choked on the words "kill Jas."

Again Beck didn't look up to see the fear in Miles. She didn't have to, she heard it. "Tell me about the day Jasmine disappeared."

"I already have. I bet you have what I said in that file," he said wearily. Now she looked up, her demeanor changed. She was in her zone, prosecutor. "You haven't told me, Mr. Gordon. Tell me what you said to those irrelevant people." He found himself obeying her.

"Jas went to shoot hoops like she always does, she's a damn good rebounder, too. Folks saw a black sedan, American model was cruisin' the area. The driver was a white guy wearing a baseball cap."

"And?"

"And? Damn woman? What's a white guy doin' cruisin' around here?"

"They're sure the driver was white?" Beck asked.

Miles was used to clueless white people. Their stupidity always pissed him off, but then he realized that was a waste of his life. Why should they get it? Their lives weren't touched by poverty and violence. They came to the projects to contribute to the poverty and the violence because the only reason they were there was for some illegal transaction. She awakened the anger in him because she was supposed to be different. She was a prosecutor. She knew what it was like in the projects.

"As sure as I am that Wilder sent a whiter than white rookie to find my daughter." Miles voice was bumping next to rage.

"I didn't hear just about anything you said, can you repeat it?" Miles glared at her.

Beck looked up from her still pen. "That's it? That's the description? Some white guy in the ubiquitous baseball cap in a black car?"

"The car had four doors," he answered derisively.

Beck nodded. "Well great, what could be easier than finding a guy in America wearing a baseball cap in a four door sedan?"

Miles leaned forward. "I know about you. I read how you lost that big case. I'm thinking Wilder sent you here to get some publicity, to show their generosity to us poor folk, or maybe you're looking to get yourself straight and important again."

Beck dug the point of the pen deep into her palm. She didn't feel the skin break, or see the pink blood and black ink mix, but Miles noticed. He saw a woman riddled with quirks and pain, but at her core there was steel. From the minute she sat down he kept thinking of a Pit Bull's jaws, how they don't release their prey. Sometimes they have to be given ammonia capsules, or pry their jaws with sticks to make them let go. She was a Pit Bull; she was what he needed to get his daughter home.

Beck mechanically put her things back in her bag. She stood up, Miles remained seated.

"I am leaving now to find a white guy in a hat. And yes, Mr. Gordon, I did fuck up the LeMond case, that rapist, son of—and yes, maybe getting Jasmine home might help me. I hope so, but as to becoming important again that would mean there was a time in my life I was important. There's no evidence of that. Mr. Gordon, I promise to keep you up to date, and I will do everything to end the hellish thoughts you've had of Jasmine ending up in a sandbox."

Miles lowered his head. He had to do battle with that image every moment of his waking day. This time Beck looked at him directly. "I will scour this city to find her and not just for you. Jasmine and I need to have a long talk about Rodman and this whole North Korean fuck up."

Miles didn't look at her but she heard a soft chuckle. Beck left. When he heard the door close, he picked up the picture of Jasmine in the jersey. "I think that crazy woman just might get you home baby." Miles hugged all he had of his daughter; his reason for being.

Seven

Homicide divisions are depressing. This one was even more so. The fluorescent lights that hung in ice cube tray fixtures cast a grey hue on the exhausted furniture and peeling paint. Every molecule of the room was infused with mourning and rage from victims and assailants. The ghastly effect of the old lights made everyone appear guilty. A constant summer drizzle accentuated the grime on the windows that were thick with condensation on the inside. There was no chance of seeing out of that sealed casket of a room. The only tie to an outside world was the clamor of a pissed off city whose railing at the world seeped its way into the dreary office. It was homicide's soundtrack.

Will's desk was crammed into a dark corner. Behind his chair a large bulletin board put him in half shadow. A sign on the board read: *For man has closed himself up, till he sees things thro' narrow chinks of his cavern.* Wm. Blake. Below the sign were crime scene photographs of the dead girl and the sand box.

Hunched over his messy desk, Will swayed to the music streaming through earphones as he read. He jumped when a file flopped down on a stack of papers in front of him. Beck was already over at the bulletin board looking at the photographs before he figured out she was there.

"Thank God," she groaned.

Will turned to her. She was taking off her sweatshirt revealing a wet, slightly transparent T-shirt. Will took a moment to appreciate Mother Nature's contribution to his day before he spoke to her. "Thank God? What the hell do you mean by that?"

"I mean she's not Jasmine Gordon, and I know how that sounds." Beck sat in a metal chair across from his desk, pointed to the file she brought.

"I need to know if Diana Gordon was arrested for anything other than prostitution. Drugs, theft, stuff that a pimp could use as leverage. Who knows, maybe Diana put her daughter in danger. She wouldn't be the first prostitute to rent her kid out to pay off a debt. No cops are going to help me, and since you said, you know."

"I said I would help. Help not an easy word for you? I'm so flattered to be your last resort," Will said lightly.

She held up her fore and middle fingers. "In case you didn't know, this means peace."

"Oldman? Were you at Woodstock?" he asked in mock seriousness.

Beck folded her forefinger, left the middle at attention. Will laughed.

A couple of detectives walked past them, did a double take when they recognized Beck. If scowls were fire, Beck would have been incinerated.

Will called out, "Hey Jim, you look like you could use some antacid."

The older, beefy detective raised his hand and furled Will the same salute Beck had.

Beck's body gyrated as her foot rocked back and forth. It was harder being back than she thought it would be. She and the detective once had a good working relationship. His hatred stung, even now. Betrayal does that, they were each guilty of it. Beck guided Will's attention back to the bulletin board. "That girl's the same age as Jasmine."

Will touched the file Beck brought. "How did your client afford a private detective, especially Wilder?"

"Pro bono, my brilliant idea has made Safra's money even more important to the agency."

Will sat on the edge of the desk, his long legs almost touched Beck. "I hope this doesn't piss you off, but I don't understand why you would work with a creep like Safra. Screw his charities and fake philanthropy; they're a blind that he displays like shiny objects for the dumb and greedy. You're neither."

"Thanks for the letting me know I'm not a greedy bastard. Tell me about her." Beck threw a paper clip at the board.

Will scanned the squad room, the gossip about Beck's presence was replaced by serious work. Will could bring down his guard. He was surprised that he held such protective feelings for Beck. It felt to good care like that, like he had for his sister. "She's fourteen, a Jane Doe. Butchered isn't the right word, even though her genitals were cut and her fingertips severed. There was a doll next to her. This part has been kept quiet. There was a streak of the victim's blood drawn between the legs and a white flower was placed there.

"God. No one has still called about a missing girl?"

Will stood up. "You know how it is, people think that the cops are their enemy and a lot of the time they're right so they don't wake the monster."

Beck cringed. "Keep calling cops monsters and the enemy, your brothers in blue will give you an honorary ring in Hell right next to me."

"Then I'll be in good company." Beck fought it but she couldn't hide that she liked the compliment. To hide her feelings she spoke in her seasoned prosecutor's voice. "Your case and mine are connected by race, age, and gender. One black girl murdered, one black girl missing. The fact this is not being screamed from the rafters is nothing short of negligence. Why hasn't this department gone to the media?"

Will smirked. "You can thank your boss for stopping that train. He really pissed off Downtown. That fucking reward, the Press. Safra hiring an agency was the same as hanging an incompetent sign on the Halls of Justice. No public official is about to sound the alarm that we know nothing about who or why a girl was dumped in the park after someone slaughtered her."

"You're right about the reward. Undo the rest. Show the city that the PD cares about African American children, that murder is murder and missing kids need to be looked for."

Will was frustrated. "No way Downtown will let me go to the Press, they have their fatheads up their collective ass."

Beck dragged her chair close to Will, spoke in a low voice. "I have a friend, Kate Taylor. She is the anchor on Channel 13 and she has the show, Focus. She'll put us on. What do you say about administering a laxative to those assholes?"

Will smiled. "Ohhh, I do like a woman who talks pretty. By the way, did that Mickey Mouse operation give you a card yet?"

Beck caught herself staring into Will's intense, blue eyes. No response.

"Well, did they?" he pushed.

"Did they? Huh, oh, did they, yeah. Not only a card but a stupid phone. Why?"

He held his hand out. Beck dug around her backpack, finally got a card.

"See, now that I have this, I can contact you."

Beck grabbed the card, wrote a number on it. "Yeah, well try my home number before you call that cell, at least at night, and don't text me or instant me until you call me at that number first."

"Can I call you at night?"

"Jesus, kid, I don't want you to break curfew or keep you up past your bedtime." Before Will could fire back his phone rang.

"Blake here." The color from his face drained as he listened. "Yeah, thanks, I'll be right over." Beck knew that he was the recipient of some hellish news.

"That was Rich. An African American girl was just reported missing. Her name is Tamara Hughes, thirteen. I gotta go."

Beck grabbed Will by the sleeve, slightly panicked. "That goddamn Harvey, the minute he knew about Jane Doe he said that she was only the first one. Will, we got to do that show. I'm calling Kate as soon as I get out of here."

Will nodded. "You're right. I'll call you later."

***

Graffiti is urban art. Urban is the city, the projects, it is also code for Black, African American and male. Embedded in the word is the legacy and the contemporary current of racism. Graffiti is art created in stealth, in the shadows. One's art is another's vandalism. Art born out of anger and suppression explodes from people who have to express what it's like to be sealed inside their skins. This is night art. Blight revealing blight.

The black sedan idled across from a building graced or denigrated by an unfinished painting of a half-dressed black woman. Red, long finger nails spread over her mouth, her back arched. A white male depicted sitting on a chair watching her. Next to the building a man handed a very young black girl a wad of cash. They turned down a corner. The sedan's engine roared as it made a U-Turn, leaving skid marks it in its wake.

***

Beck's constant pacing was evidenced by a deep path she created in the maroon Persian carpet. A single track showed little trace of the intricate pattern or startling rich colors the rest of the rug boasted. The track was a perfectly straight line. Even when she was losing it, Beck's clinical need for control manifested itself in some oblique way. On the TV Michael Jordan, the 1998 version, soared unearthly heights to slam the basketball in the swaying net. Beck stopped her monomaniacal pacing to rewind the videotape, not a DVD, a tape. She stopped it to where a green and black haired Dennis Rodman knocked the Utah Jazz's Karl Malone to the floor, who then grabbed Rodman's leg, and down the court they wrestled. Beck stopped the video, rewound to the exact same spot a couple of times. She put it on pause when the phone rang, then waited for the machine to do its job. Beck harbored a sadistic thrill knowing that the hapless caller had no cue when to speak or that the amount of time to speak was not enough to leave more than the caller's name.

Harvey was a pro getting what he wanted recorded. He knew Beck worked hard to avoid human contact. The anger in his voice revealed he was in no mood for Beck's issues. I'm your boss, answer now," he commanded.

Beck turned off the TV, stared at the track in the rug. She put one foot outside of it, lost her balance for a moment. Anger generated by Harvey revived her equilibrium. She sprinted to the phone.

"You son of a bitch. How dare you let Safra involve me in your televised freak show?" She spied an old bottle of beer between boxes marked TV Network Shopping. She took a swig of the stale, flat liquid.

"You think I wanted you on the Safra case?" Harvey exploded. "I had no damn clue he was pulling that. I begged him to take you off the case, reminded him that not only do the cops hate you but so does the Press; but he said it is either you or he walks from the agency."

Beck tracked the groove as she spoke. "Why me?"

"He's a fan, said he watched you in court."

"That's bullshit, you think I would have missed his steroid bloated entourage? He's up to something, Harvey."

"When isn't he up to something? You find Richard Safra's only child, then none of us will ever have to work again. You can buy your own shopping network. He will demand to meet you, so when he summons you, be on time and appropriately dressed."

Beck drained the last of the disgusting beer. "Appropriate? Five people asked me where my Bible was. Your fashion days are done. What do you know about Detective Will Blake?"

A long sigh preceded Harvey's frustrated tone. "That pain in the ass. He should worry you and I'm worried that he's the only cop who will spend five minutes with you."

"Well, that pain in the ass and I are going on Kate's show tomorrow night to talk about Jasmine, the Jane Doe, and oh God, Harvey, another kid has gone missing. Did you know that?"

No response. "Harvey, Harvey?"

"I was just thinking about the free publicity. You need to lay the pro bono on thick and heavy."

"That's your response?" Beck hung up. Ten seconds it rang again. This time she grabbed the receiver right away "Yes, jerk off."

"Excuse me?" Beck squatted, balanced on the balls of her feet. "Will? Great. This is why I shouldn't answer the phone."

"You could say hello. Here, I will do it, hello Beck. See, like that."

Beck struggled with a quip, but it wasn't coming. Will changed his tone. "Harvey was right. We're in the beginning of some real sick shit. We need to talk in person. Can you meet me tomorrow morning for coffee at Rudy's?"

"Okay, when?" She asked in the same serious tone.

"Umm, six-thirty. I've heard you're not a morning person. Just so you know, I will be armed. Good night."

Beck scrunched herself into a fetal position, lay across the groove in the carpet.

"Please, don't let me be too late to help Jasmine and Miles, please."

***

Beck stumbled into the insanely busy coffee shop exactly at six-thirty. Not a single hair on her head met a brush that morning. Her unnecessary sunglasses and hoodie obscured her face. Her sweats were at least three sizes too big. She was a mess.

Will's back faced her, but his long, blue black hair was unmistakable. Beck worked her way through the maze of tables occupied by sleepy, irritated people. When she finally got to Will, her ill temper was worsened by the fact Will had coffee, but no cup was waiting for her. She didn't have to say a word. Will did not need to see the rest of her face. The vibes were clear. He shoved his cup to her.

"I want my own cup." Beck shoved it back to him. Will waved to a server, pointed to his cup indicated another one, quickly. Finally she sat down.

"Why here? Why so ridiculously early? This place is not close to where you work or where I live?" Beck barely finished the sentence as the coffee, in record time, was placed in front of her.

Will understood he should speak as little as possible until Beck woke up. He slid a file to her. She didn't even see it until she slugged down several gulps of scalding coffee.

Now she could focus. She went through the autopsy photographs impassively. "Jane Doe's genitals were excised, what the hell does that mean? Any theories about the missing fingertips, other than he takes trophies? Kids aren't finger printed unless they've been in trouble, well at least kids in the projects. Jesus. He bathed her, washed her hair and brushed her teeth. That's not about hiding evidence, that's something else." Beck's calmness was replaced by apprehension.

Will nodded. "This is a very particular, tedious ritual. We have one dead girl and two missing. Maybe we should put Safra's kid in the mix."

Beck disagreed. "She's been gone for weeks, plus she is wealthy, in her twenties. She's biracial but that's not enough of a connection. She doesn't fit the profile of Jane Doe and Jasmine." Beck voice thinned to a whisper after she spoke Jasmine's name.

Will's face expressed disagreement. "Maybe. I'm not sure Safra should be discounted," he said sharply. His tenor surprised him. He modulated as he continued. "The longer they're not found, the higher the chance they're dead. You're right about going on TV. Besides getting the word out, it might make some things more, more manageable."

Will pretended to drink coffee to avoid speaking.

Beck tried to get a bead on what was making him squirm. "What things need to be more manageable?" Beck's tone was accusatory.

Will continued to drink, his eyes were downcast. Beck did not take her eyes off of him. It was not in her personality to let anyone off the hook. She sat back into her chair, took off her sun glasses. She wasn't sure if his shocked expression was a reaction to her puffy eyes, underscored by black circles, or that he realized she knew what he was going to say before he did.

He spoke very slowly. "Since your visit to the station, I've been bombarded with what started as unsolicited avuncular advice that turned in to veiled threats that has become ultimatums about working with you."

Beck didn't move. She didn't even blink. When she spoke her lips barely moved. "I thought you said you thought I got screwed."

Will nodded. "Yes, I did, I do. I think the whole LeMond thing was bullshit...from what I know."

Beck cocked her head to the side when he said "from what I know." That was it. She shoved the table hard, the coffee cup fell over. The black liquid was like a waterfall pooling on the floor. Every nerve in her body fired. She scanned the café, strategized the fastest route out.

"I get why we're here so early. You didn't want to take the chance that anyone would see us together. I guess I was supposed to sit here and plead with you, assure you that I'm not any of those things the good old boys in blue say I am. Well, sorry, because I am every lousy thing they say I am and more. Now that you know that, are you going on TV? You know what, don't answer me. You show, you show."

Beck pushed more than a few intimidated people out of the way to exit the café.

Will slowly turned the cup right side up, attempted to sop up the liquid with a disintegrating napkin.

Beck ran to the closest bus stop bench. Her face streamed with sweat. She pulled off her sweatshirt down to a sports bra, buried her head into the shirt, screamed primal angst.

****

Richard Safra's office was the personification of the man. Cold, secretive. It was built to the specifications of an ornate mausoleum. Safra believed corpses were beautiful, even alluring. Those who died young were particularly lucky. Their sins could never be traced on their faces perfected by the mortician's artistry. The corpse was a twisted incarnation of the fountain of youth. What was most beautiful to him was that a corpse held the answer to the best kept secret, death. All of the things he treasured in a corpse were his own character traits. Cold, bloodless, and the holder of many secrets related to death.

The room was like his wealth, massive. Every ornament was a symbol, a warning to heed his wealth and power. They were reminders to those who entered to tread lightly, an invaluable survival skill. What was not on display was a single picture of a human being, most notably, no picture of Olivia Safra.

The blinds covering the massive floor to ceiling windows were closed. The room was pitch black with the exception of a remote corner lit by the luminescent light that emanated from a theatrical sized TV. Cradled in a sumptuous sofa, Safra watched Beck on the screen. She had the look of someone being hunted as she walked through a gauntlet of reporters. A voice narrated the scene. "Assistant District Attorney, Rebekkah Oldman, has been suspended from her duties after the high profile sexual abuse case brought against the Mayor's assistant Jack LeMond was dismissed due to a bad search ordered by Oldman." A reporter jammed a microphone into her face. Beck's expression shifted from the hunted to the hunter. Safra paused the scene. He walked to the TV, with a steady finger he traced the outline of Beck's frozen face.

Eight

Kate Taylor sat on the arm of a tired loveseat as she skillfully put on the last touches of the perfect nude lipstick on her perfect anchorwoman mouth. She filled the bill of attractiveness that is demanded for anchorwomen while their male counterparts are allowed to become fat, old, and often are in desperate need of a new hairpiece. Kate's cascade of blond hair couldn't hide her best trait, her intelligence. Yet, with all of that she never made it to the major leagues of news. The makeup room at the small station had three chairs, a cracked mirror, and one makeup artist who looked fourteen, maybe. After Kate took the last swipe at a hair that had not been out of place, she focused her attention on her best friend who was being her usual self. Beck was difficult in new situations and she was almost impossible in the makeup chair. The almost was out of the equation when she was told by the unsuspecting girl that she had learned her craft online.

"You learned how to apply makeup on people online, how?" Beck demanded.

"They sent us pictures of faces to download and we practiced on them. We sent their pictures to the teachers," she said timidly.

Kate was a little horrified that she let this kid do her makeup but was more concerned by Beck, the eternal prosecutor. Kate had to save the girl from a withering cross examination that was about to convene, but Beck was too swift. "You practiced on paper? You colored on paper, with what, crayons, and that makes you a…?" That was it. Kate guided the frightened girl out of the room to safety.

Beck was about to scrub off the girl's artistry but the fact was she had achieved a soft, lovely brightness on Beck's face, a brightness that belied the darkness churning inside her. She had stopped thinking of Jasmine as living. Kate patted Beck's shoulder.

"Beck, she did a good job. You got to cut people some slack Oldman, especially yourself. That detective better get here soon. If he doesn't show, the whole segment goes to Olivia Safra's case."

Beck stared at Kate in the mirror. "Two black girls are missing, another one's dead. They're not news worthy over one rich girl with or without the PD?"

"No, Beck, not in this market, they're not." Kate spat out the words because she hated the truth they held. She realized a long time ago how ironic it was that she was a reporter who hated to tell ugly facts. But she was good at it, blunt, like Beck. It was one of the reasons they were so close.

"Then talk about Olivia, but you won't. No one does. The story is always about Daddy." Beck expected Kate to argue back, but she had stopped listening the minute she saw Will walking towards the makeup room.

"My God, Beck, now I see your interest in these cases."

"Am I in the right spot for makeup?" Will asked. Kate extended her hand along with her sexiest smile. "Kate Taylor."

"Detective William Blake, Will. I really appreciate your doing this segment," he said.

"Take a seat Detective and it's you who should be thanked. My rude friend shares my gratitude. She terrified the little makeup girl, so I am going to try and coax her back for you. Beck, if I get the kid back here, don't say a word to her, not one syllable."

Beck glowered at Kate until she exited. It was the first time Beck saw Will dressed like a homicide detective in a jacket and tie. She didn't swoon, exactly. Damn, why did he have to be so great looking? Will took a half step toward her chair.

"Blake wrote that what is grand is necessarily obscure to weak men. I finally understood what that meant today. Those men who warned me about you have no ability to see you for who you are. They're limited by codes and skewed ideas of loyalty. They follow these things blindly and it has made them weak. I need to talk to you, tell you what I wanted to say this morning but didn't."

Just as Beck's face showed a glimmer of humanity, the girl stood at the threshold. Beck's bird of prey demeanor reappeared. It was a reflex that she knew she had to control.

"They need you on the set and I need to work on him," the girl said. Then she looked at Will. "God, why do you need makeup?"

Beck got up to give Will the chair but the girl bolted. "Guess she can't see my grandness either." Will smiled. "I'll have Kate get her, but she's right, I don't know what she can improve on." Beck couldn't believe she gave Will a compliment. She exited faster than the makeup girl.

Beck found Kate at the news desk. The camera, lights, and crew were ready.

"Jesus, Beck that Will." He arrived before Kate could finish. He sat next to Beck.

The director signaled a five count.

"Welcome to Focus On The City. We begin our program with a grim subject, the disappearance of young girls in our city. My guests are William Blake, homicide detective, and Rebekkah Oldman, a former assistant district attorney, now a private detective for the Wilder Agency who is working on the Olivia Safra case."

"Ms. Taylor," interrupted Beck. "We aren't here for the Safra case which has already received an enormous amount of media coverage. We're here to bring attention to three African American girls. The Wilder agency has taken a pro bono missing person case. Jasmine Gordon is thirteen-years-old. She was last seen shooting hoops in her neighborhood, on the second of June."

Beck held up a picture of Jasmine to the wrong camera.

Annoyed, Kate moved her hand to the correct position. "Yes, as I was going to say, you and Detective Blake are working together."

"Wait, what, no, Ms. Oldman and I are not working together exactly. We're sharing information. I have a homicide case of an unidentified adolescent African American girl."

Will's interruption after Beck's exasperated Kate. She knew their time was limited. They needed to let her guide them. Will continued.

"We know nothing about the girl who was found in Chelsea Park. We don't believe she was murdered in the park. She was brought there. She was placed with objects that at this time I am not going to disclose. This girl was mutilated. In addition to

Jasmine Gordon, another girl, Tamara June Hughes was reported missing yesterday. She lives close to the park which is situated near Jasmine's neighborhood." As Will took a breath to continue, Kate jumped in.

"You're implying that these cases are connected, please expand on that," Kate commanded.

Will didn't want to expand. It meant he would be giving the green light to a serial killer theory. He was not ready, nor did he have the authority to pose the theory. He wanted to leave the implication. His silence turned the director into a madman, gesticulating for one of them to speak.

"What I am saying is that we need to identify the body of Jane Doe. We need to hear from someone who knew her."

Kate exhibited the perfect faux sincere TV smile to Beck. She had to ask the question that no one wanted asked. "Ms. Oldman, if these girls have some connection, is it much of a stretch to wonder if Olivia Safra's disappearance could be linked?"

It was hard to gauge who was more pissed off by Kate, Beck or Will, but Will spoke first.

"Seriously, that's where you're going? Safra?" How much coverage does that one person get? I mean of course his daughter's disappearance is important, but we're here for three children. There has not been one major news story about a brutally murdered African American child. Nothing from you guys, or on the Internet, nothing. Only a few lines on the crime page in a newspaper pretty much nobody buys."

Beck nodded her head as if she were keeping time to her favorite song.

Kate arched her back, desperately tried to look professional and not like a deer caught in the klieg lights.

The director ran up as close as he could, slashed his throat with his finger indicating Will should stop. This only incited him.

"African American parents need to watch their kids very closely, especially your girls. We are in long hot summer nights. There's no school and the weather is making staying inside hell. The kids are on the streets, and so is a dangerous person looking for them. Call your local politician; don't let the phone stop ringing at the police precincts. Please contact us if your daughter, niece, grandchild or neighbor is missing."

Kate signaled the director, immediately the camera was on her.

"Thank you so much Detective Blake and Ms. Oldman. Our time has come to an end. We are running the phone number of the Wilder Agency on the crawl and you can find it on our webpage. Of course, contact the police with any information you may have. Thanks for watching and stay focused."

Instantly the lights softened. The three people didn't move or speak as they absorbed what just happened. Kate gawked at Will.

"Do you know the shit storm you've just caused? You just freaked out the city. Not to mention pissed off your superiors." Will's voice shook with frustration.

"If those girls had blue hair and blond eyes, you know what I mean, their parents would have their own network. But poor kids, black kids, who gives a shit, right?"

"Will," Beck said, calmly, "Kate's on our side."

"Yeah, shit, I'm just so tired of this." Will sounded weary.

"No worries, Detective. You have a lot more to be concerned about than my little ol' feelings. You just touched the last nerve of every cop and politician in the city," said Kate sympathetically." Beck nodded.

"Downtown is going to hand you your head on used toilet paper," Beck said matter-of-factly.

"Kate, your friend sure knows how to turn a phrase," Will said drily. Kate rolled her eyes in agreement.

Will put his arm around Kate's shoulders, "I know I've caused you to catch some heat."

"Didn't Beck tell you," Kate rejoined, "I love tropical climates?"

Even from across the studio, they felt the wrath coming from the director. Kate fanned her face as if she were sweating. "Beck, wait for me by the dressing room. Detective, I wish you good luck. Let's hope our careers don't end up in the obituaries tomorrow." Kate directed her angry boss away from them.

"I really like your friend Beck," Will began. "About this morning, I started it out wrong. You were so wiped out-- okay, take two. What I mean, what I mean is this: I don't care about what those assholes say. The wall of blue is that, a wall. Walls don't think or adapt. I want to help you find Jasmine. We know the cases are connected. We can help each other. I have to go now, but we'll talk later, okay?"

Beck stared down at her feet like an awkward adolescent. Finally she nodded. Will squeezed her hand which made her look up, smiling, sort of. Will passed Kate on her way back to Beck. Kate leaned against the wall, admiring Will until he disappeared around the corner.

"Beck, if you don't follow up on that, then I will be sending thee to the nunnery."

"Shit, Kate, he's twelve."

"My dear he's old enough to nod his head in compliance, that's all that matters." Beck shoved Kate, laughing in agreement.

***

Motels. Lurid, repellant establishments that evoke fear, shame, and family memories. Without the innocence, lurid has nothing going for it. Dark rooms. Flickering TV's. Voices that do not carry the cadence of the psychologically well-adjusted; laughter not connected to humor. These unsavory sounds bleed through paper thin walls. They're the subliminal soundtrack as families eat greasy chicken and fries and recount the day at the amusement park. Parents tell their children that the rhythmic pounding on the wall is a game played by the occupants of the next room. Motels are inhabited by loners who contemplate ghastly deeds done to themselves, or others; lonely people who travel for a living or to create distance from their own lives. People rest their heads on pillows encased in human secretion and secrets. The rooms run in a straight line, connecting depravity to the banal. What all occupants have in common is the wish that their lives afforded hotel accommodations. Motels are made up of people connected by secrets, transience, and budgets. If the people with ice cream wishes and summer memories only knew how close they were to someone who made them put dead bolts on their doors and security systems in their homes. If they only knew that in the room next door, separated by cheap plaster and a crumby painting sat a person whose deeds may be depicted in a cheesy TV movie. A movie about a killer who no one saw because he looked so normal at the motel pool.

The TV flickered in room 232 at the Happy Haven Motel. On screen was the Focus TV program. The light cast a strange hue on the turquoise painted walls. The blond woman on screen appeared rattled as she bid farewell. The guests were familiar, at least the interesting woman with the short hair. The annoying crawl zipped by but not too fast to miss the words Wilder Agency and a telephone number. CLICK, no sound. Now just images emanated from the set. The light in the bathroom came on; it was the only light besides the glow from the TV. The door was half closed. A perfect slice of illumination from the bathroom highlighted a baseball cap that lay sideways on the cheap bedspread. Next to the cap was a case of utensils, not knives exactly, more like surgical instruments. The blades were clean, but their shine was dulled by the shadowy room. The bathroom door opened wider, allowing for more of the yellow light to enter the room. Steam from the hot shower floated over the bed and over to the dresser where a carefully aligned set of white stuffed animals rested. The yellow light muddied the white fur on the kittens, puppies, and lambs. White artificial flowers, candles, and unclothed baby dolls were jaundiced by the motel light. A light that changed the innocent into the lurid.

Nine

Harvey Wilder smiled, rarely. He never beamed, beaming was not in his DNA. What he was when Beck walked into his office was triumphant with a dash of smugness, topped with a pinch of relief. He signaled for Beck to sit in the warm pecan colored leather chair that faced his desk. Its twin was occupied by a stack of newspapers. Harvey was old school. He hated cell phones, texts, and the assholes who took pictures of their food, then shared the relic of their inane lives on the Twitter/splitter/ shitter world, as he referred to it. He was a lot like Beck in his disdain for technology that usurped the human mind. He and Beck shared that philosophy, good for chats over cocktails, but that's where it ended. Harvey lived in the real world, not on its fringe, where philosophers and people with problems like Beck dwelled. Harvey wanted money, lots of it. Beck didn't know how much she earned; she just knew it was enough to live. On that point Harvey never failed to point out to Beck that she lived well. So Harvey used the devices to stay current and flush even though his heart belonged to inked, cursive (the mark of the educated) writings. When there was a story about him or the agency, he bought the paper in bundles. Clearly, from the stacks, his name was in print.

Ms. Pitt entered the room bearing two steaming cups of coffee on a tray with a pitcher of cream, sugar, and pastries. She made no eye contact with Beck, made no sound whatsoever; her presence and disappearance occurred without comment.

"Adolescent African American girl, blah, blah, case is being investigated PRO BONO, (Harvey's voice boomed) by Wilder Investigations. Wait, generously investigated. How did I miss that word? By God Beck, your TV debut was a hit, a hit I tell you. Wilder Agency, the company with a heart. Fucking great." Harvey poured a generous dollop of cream into a mug, shoved half a cheese Danish into his mouth. While he was not beaming, there was an aura about him. On the other hand, Beck was, well, Beck. She was annoyed by the ooey glob of cheese excreted onto the side of Harvey's greedy mouth.

"You know, Harvey, Will's responsible for you getting your rocks off from the publicity. While you're eating your way to a coronary, he's facing the weasels Downtown."

Harvey didn't hear her because he was too busy with his phone which made the human being in front of him secondary. Though Harvey complained that technology was a cause of less human interaction, he did not apply that criticism to himself. Beck was on the verge of throwing something at him.

"Jesus, they've even put Will's rant on Auto tune. It's going viral." Harvey started to show her but he couldn't stop watching.

"Blake must carry the same self-destructive gene that affects you. Telling these parents to hide their kids; the cops must want to string him up…" Harvey jumped at an explosive thud. He looked down to see a large dictionary that landed at his feet. Beck missed, she'd aimed for Harvey's head. "See that, it's called a dictionary. You might want to look up the word conscience. It is something Will demonstrated when he spoke out. He has one; you don't even know what it is." Harvey picked up the dictionary, placed it carefully back to its rightful place on his desk. "Throwing books is a sin, Beck, look it up. No matter, you cannot piss me off today Ms. Oldman. Follow me." Before Beck could barrage Harvey with a few choice retorts; he was gone.

***

Beck finally caught up with him after getting lost in the huge building. He was leaning against a wall, amused. She started to renew her frustration but stopped when she saw him wipe the name plate on the door. It read: Rebekkah Oldman: Senior Investigator. Knowing he stymied her assault, Harvey opened the door to a sun drenched, three window office. Beck started to sit in the same guest chairs that Harvey had in his office. He guided her to the desk chair. He made a sweeping gesture for her to be seated. She did, robotically. Her shock was a source of joy for Harvey. He seated himself across from her. Folded his handkerchief and pleated it carefully before he rested it in his breast pocket.

"I told you that I would take care of you, Beck, which makes me ask, what is up with you and this detective?"

Beck rubbed the fine wood of the desk, scanned the most up to date laptop and desk top computers. She smiled widely at the wall filled with law books, a relic from the long ago past of less than a decade. She knew this awe was keeping her from doing something but she didn't care for a few blissful moments. Harvey was in control, he loved the rare moment he had with her.

"Beck." She looked up, smiled at Harvey. It was a greeting that one gives after not seeing someone for a long time. Beck had forgotten how just moments earlier she was harboring homicidal thoughts against him.

"Oh, Harvey, yeah, this is some office, nothing like the one I had, wait, what did you say?"

"I asked what is with you and the junior detective," he repeated. Now Beck focused. "No, you tell me what your pals in homicide say about him," she said coyly.

Harvey crossed his legs, swatted at a nonexistent piece of lint from his trousers. Harvey was in the driver's seat. "He's intellectual, moody, arty. Half the time no one knows what the hell he's talking about. Not a team player. You know, all the crap that women go for, which I guess may make you immune."

"You're such an asshole, Harvey."

"From you, that's a compliment. Detective Blake is Ivy League, rich, very rich. He said no to all of that money or no to working with dear old Dad or maybe said no to all of it because his sister was murdered." Beck swung around to face him.

The question did not need to be voiced.

"Yes, his sister was murdered, and no, no one was arrested. The case went cold. An amateur shrink might theorize that he walked out on his cushy life to the hell of being a homicide cop because every crime he solves avenges his sister's murder. He clearly is smart, ambitious; he earned his shield fast."

It finally sunk into Harvey. He dropped his arms on either side of his chair.

"Oh come on, you're not falling for kindergarten cop. Aren't you too old for…?"

"You know what Harvey…" Beck was interrupted by the desk phone ringing.

Harvey's foot twitched with each unanswered ring. He took a pen from his pocket, flung it at Beck's head, missed, hit the back of the chair. She slowly turned to face him.

"What's with you and phones?" he asked in exasperation.

"I'm getting tired of your cracks about my age." She answered the phone

"Hello? Oh, wait, whose secretary? Mine? You're my secretary. Huh. Hi. What? Um, yes, I guess so. Sure, I'll tell Mr. Wilder, yeah, I look forward to meeting you too."

Beck leaned as far back as the chair allowed. "Richard Safra thought I was very effective on TV and wants me, and you, in his office today at six. My secretary, I have a secretary, her name is Ann. She said he has been trying to find you."

Harvey crooked his neck as if he needed to work out a kink; leaned his hands upon the desk. He spoke in a monotone, removing any hint of emotion.

"He never makes direct contact to people he hasn't been formally introduced to, never, I mean ever. Spooky. Don't be late, Beck." Harvey didn't issue an order, it was a warning.

***

The midmorning heat was miserable but the humidity was cruel torture. Beck's hair stuck to her head like a skull cap. Her underarms steamed. She sweat so much her sunglasses were in a constant freefall down her slippery nose. Each time she pushed the glasses in place, reminded her of how miserable she was. The sweat off her body sizzled as it hit the cement. Not a sliver of shade anywhere in the projects. No trees, no grass, no greenery. She stopped in a corner market for some fruit. She was pretty sure the young black woman called her stupid when she exited.

What the fuck was she thinking to ask for a kiwi? Fresh fruits and vegetables, here? The projects are also known as food deserts. Food deserts, another stupid euphemism for poverty stricken neighborhoods. Another layer of urban dwelling. She could hear Miles Gordon now. "You're not whiter than white, Oldman, you're transparent."

Though she was looking for girls playing basketball, she marveled to find them doing exactly that in the wretched heat. As she made her way to them, it felt like the black asphalt sunk under her feet. Beck looked to see if she left footprints.

Several girls dominated the court, while younger boys watched. All activity stopped as they looked at Beck. A white, sweating woman stupidly dressed in pants, long sleeves, all black. Right as she started to call to the girls, one of the boys cranked up an ancient boom box. The bass could blow out an eardrum.

The girls steeled themselves in magnificent teen "whatdayawant bitch" attitude as she approached them.

"Hey girls, I was wondering if I could speak to you for a minute."

Hands on their waists, hips splayed out, heads cocked to the side was her answer.

"I'm here about Jasmine Gordon, trying to help her dad find her."

One of the girls unlocked her hip and the attitude.

"I saw you on TV last night. Yeah, about Jasmine, she's okay." The girls circled around Beck. They were so tall they provided shade.

"Oh yeah, well, then you know why I'm here. What's your name?" she asked casually.

"Tia," answered only half bitchy.

"Tia, that's pretty. Really need some help to find Jasmine. Anything you can tell me would be great. For example, did Jasmine have any new friends, any boyfriends?"

Tia restored the attitude. "Oh, so now she's a slut."

"Whoa, whoa, who said that? No."

"If any girl around here likes a boy, she's a slut."

Another girl chuckled. "The only balls Jas cares 'bout is basketballs."

The girls laughed, including Beck.

"Yeah, smart move. After dating a few guys, you'll understand," advised Beck.

"You got that right," agreed Tia.

"Is there anything anyone can tell me, even if you already told the cops?"

They all chimed, "Cops? What cops? No one's asked us shit about Jasmine."

"You know 'bout Jas's mama?" asked Tia.

Beck nodded.

"Yeah, well, it messed her up, knowin' her mama was whorin'. A little while ago she said she got someone to talk to about how she was feelin'."

"She knew about her mother? Who told her; who is this person?" There was desperation in Beck's tone.

Everyone shook their heads. Beck tried to take notes, but the sweat dropped on her paper making the ink bleed. She got sick of keeping her glasses from falling, yanked them off so hard they flew out of her hand, shattering on the hot asphalt.

"Thought as women get the menopause they chill out," mused Kylie. Beck unclenched. She smiled, or at least thought she did, but her expression confused the girls. Tia pushed Kylie out of the way so she could speak directly to Beck.

"I thought it was weird, no it's fucked up because the person who's helping Jasmine about her mama, is the person who told her about her mama. What kind of shit is that? Hey, Jas let me tell you some really bad shit so I screw you up, then I'll give you some lame assed advice. If that's not messin' with someone, then I don't know what is."

Beck was impressed with Tia's wisdom.

Beck nodded. "Yeah, kind of made the person an instant best friend. We share something special, and have a secret from your dad. Do know where she met this person?" asked Beck.

A new group of girls arrived. They catcalled to get the game on. All but Tia left. She picked up Beck's destroyed sunglasses. Beck tried to straighten the bent frame but the glasses laid crooked on her face. Tia couldn't help but laugh. The glasses were the cherry on the top of Beck's misery sundae.

"I dunno if this means nuthin, but a couple of times when we played at night, I saw some big black car, not a cool one, just a black car parked across the street there. No one ever came over, but I thought we was being watched. It was creepy," said Tia.

Beck gave Tia a card. "If you see that car again, call me."

"You get Jas back to us, we need her." Tia ran to the other girls.

Beck watched them as she tried to straighten her damn glasses. Not a chance. She dropped them on the ground, smashed them under her shoe. She relished destroying something that had failed her.

Tia watched Beck, amused until they locked gazes. Then the humor drained away, Tia's expression communicated something else. You're scared, Beck thought, that's not enough, be terrified. Tia understood.

***

Beck sunk low in the chair across from Will's desk. Several detectives spoke in fake whispers, the "itch" at the end of bitch was loud and clear. After the second time, Beck sat straight up glared at the men until they moved out of earshot. Jim hadn't noticed her at first. When he did, he made a B line to her.

"You haven't done enough to the cops in this house? Now it's his turn to be screwed? Blake's a kid and my partner, mostly. How the hell could you let him cut off his own balls on TV? A stupid move and departmental suicide. You've a knack for letting people take the fall for you," Jim growled.

"Hey Jim, what's going on?" Jim didn't turn when Will spoke to him. "We warned you Blake, we tried." Jim didn't join the other detectives when he left.

"Jim's hatred for me is greater than all of the others put together. He has his reasons, Will."

"He chooses to be blind, remember?" admonished Will.

"Oohh, right. Listen, I found out that Jasmine got a brand new friend. Someone became her new BFF by sharing news that her mother was a whore. Now she needed someone to talk to about this, but who? The person who inflicted the pain. Her father has no idea that Jasmine knew about her mother. He has no idea his daughter kept a secret from him. A secret refuses to be lonely. It has to have company which makes me wonder what else Jasmine didn't tell Miles."

Will laced his hands behind his neck. "How did this person know about her mother, a customer? A pissed off neighbor? Did anyone see this person?"

"No, no one has a clue who it is." Beck mindlessly picked up a pencil, tapped it against her forehead as if the drumming could awaken something.

"Well, we just found out who Jane Doe is." Beck stopped the drumming.

"Her name is Camille Davis, fifteen, just turned. Her grandmother saw the show. This grandmother is your age."

Beck's expression of curiosity switched to an unmistakable look of "fuck you."

"Oh, no, come on, I didn't mean; she's too damn young to be a grandmother is my point, Beck. Camille's father is in prison, her mother's dead. She lives with her grandmother. They fight constantly because Camille is sexually active and Grandma knows what it's like to be a teen mom."

Beck did not respond. He forged on. "She works two fast food jobs. She has to be out of the house at least eighteen hours a day, so she can't be around to monitor homework, let alone track Camille down after each fight. There is nothing out of the ordinary for Camille to disappear after some big knock down fight. That's why no calls."

"A kid was found dead. And does this woman have a name, beyond Grandma? Beck asked coolly.

"Yes, she does. Naomi. Her name is Naomi and Naomi told me in very clear, precise terms that she thinks cops are corrupt assholes. Her son is in prison on a pot charge. I mean come on, if her son were white, no prison, no nothing. I don't blame people for not calling us unless it is a bare bones need."

"Well, bones are all that's left." Beck hated what she said. So did Will, but the fact was no matter how crudely she put it, it was correct.

Jim walked past Beck, blocked her view of Will. "They found the Gordon kid. She's dead, and cut up like the Davis girl. You need to get there, Blake." Jim handed Will a piece of paper. As he left, he couldn't resist one last look of hatred aimed at Beck, but she couldn't see it. She couldn't focus on anything except the voice in her head screaming that she had killed Jasmine.

"Oh God, oh shit, not again not again not again, what have I done, what have I done?" she howled.

"Stop it. You've done nothing, Beck." Beck's eyes were blank as if all the life had just been snuffed out. She responded with an eerie calmness. "Exactly, I did nothing." Then she moved robotically, gathered her things, walked slowly to the exit.

***

It was mid-afternoon but it looked like night. Heavily weighted clouds blocked even the tiniest ray of sunshine. Endless drizzle and humidity saturated everyone. A few intrepid protestors forged on. They carried signs that read EQUAL PROTECTION FOR BLACK CHILDREN but on many the black ink bled, elongating the words, making the sign's appearance grotesque. The media was well represented as were the ever present contingency of people who were thrilled by the idea of murder. Their lust to see the body of a murder victim was insatiable.

Will and Beck moved swiftly to the barricades that blocked the front of the church. An officer saw his badge, motioned him forward. As they moved past, he pointed to the protestors.

"Thanks for this, Blake." A reporter heard his name, shouted at Will which started a chorus of questions. They moved to the back of the church, away from the din. They followed the cops and crime scene investigators to a small fenced garden that was lit up like a sound stage. The tarps over the grave fluttered. Emily was at the scene. In each hand she held a clear evidence bag. One contained a white stuffed puppy, the other white, fake flowers. Lilies of the field. She smiled at Will.

"Blake, we gotta stop meeting like this."

Emily noticed Beck, but couldn't make out who she was because Beck stared up at the dark sky. Finally Emily realized that this was the infamous Rebekkah Oldman. A surge of anger shot through her. She watched Beck who was disconnected from the chaos that surrounded the scene. Emily had no desire to greet the traitor. She addressed Will.

"Go ahead Blake. We got most of what we need. I'll be right back. Oh, only authorized personnel." She pointed to Beck.

"I authorize her," Will said sharply.

Emily shrugged. Will and Beck entered the crime scene. Beck walked ahead of Will.

There she was. The face Beck had seen in photo after photo in Miles Gordon's home. A shallow grave had been dug among the zucchini and the roses. Jasmine looked asleep. The only thing that gave away her actual state was the plastic bag on each hand. Emily stood behind them.

"Her fingertips were cut off. Very similar to Chelsea Park. Fingertips, genital mutilation. The offerings."

"Offerings?" asked Will.

"The stuffed animal, flowers, a candle, doll. What else would you call that stuff? She's been dead about thirty, thirty-six hours. There is one important difference, the cause of death. Camille Davis bled out. This girl was strangled. Plus, this seems more, I dunno, messy. I mean her underwear is new, she's bathed, but her hair is damp, not combed. I can't put my finger on it, but things seem rushed," Emily mused.

Beck nodded her head wildly in agreement; she was now fully connected to what was happening

"Of course it's rushed. The bastard panicked; panicked when he saw us on TV. It was my brilliant idea to go on TV, didn't even think that it may make him feel corned. I failed another kid. I told Harvey. I told him."

Beck paced. Will tried to keep an eye her as he spoke to Emily. "God, working with Oldman, that's what I call hard labor, Blake," Emily said contemptuously.

Will wrote down the last of his notes. Turned to Emily, ready to lay her out for her remark when he realized that Beck was gone. A single clap of a thunder preceded the torrential rain.

***

Beck's apartment was dark. A slip of light sneaked its way through the one speck of the window that wasn't covered. She spoke on the phone in a voice thickened by anger and pain.

"What's your special deal of the day? I want five of them—yes, gas weed cutters. How is that any of your fucking business? Too bad. You wouldn't hear that language if you just did your job without the meaningless--I already gave you my information. Really, a nice day?"

Beck scrunched her knees to her chest, rested her head for just a moment. She was sorry she took the shit of the world out on some poor woman who answered a phone all day long. She turned off the TV, walked to her bedroom. She caught her reflection as she walked by a mirror; she flipped herself off, then turned the mirror side to the wall. Beck crawled onto the unmade bed. The only light in the room came from the green numbers on the digital clock which read three fifteen.

The incessant ringing of the phone finally aroused Beck from her death sleep. She saw the time, five forty-six. She threw her arm over her forehead head, thinking, trying to remember. It finally came back to her with a chill, Safra.

***

Beck dragged herself to Ms. Pitt's desk. She interpreted Pitt's expression as just her constant state of hate and loathing for her, but this time Beck misread the look.

Pitt was engrossed by the trace of lipstick smeared over Beck's lips just enough to make her think of the Joker. She quelled a snicker when she saw the red moccasins, was overjoyed by Beck's dripping hair. But what gave Pitt her deepest thrill was that this nightmare was late again, and this time too late for redemption. Just as she was going to let Harvey know of Beck's arrival, she barged into his office. Sometimes, Pitt thought, life could not be more perfect.

Beck collapsed in a chair. She didn't notice the fury that distorted Harvey's face.

"Harvey, Jasmine, I just…" Harvey's voice cut her thought. "What a piece of work you are. You're late, today, of all days."

"Yeah of all days. The day that Jasmine was found butchered and strangled to death. She was left in a church garden. I think that's at least a step above a sandbox, right? Not that you care, but you should because it means I don't work for you anymore. Dead kid, case closed. I'm not on your clock."

There was a movement from a darkened corner of the large office. Richard Safra appeared as if he walked out of a veil of mist. Beck was ready to continue, to switch her anger to Safra, except Harvey forgot about Beck. He looked at Safra as if he were a ghost.

"Richard, I thought you left a long time ago," he gasped.

Safra glided past Harvey as if he were not a corporeal presence. He invaded Beck's personal space, put his arm on her shoulders. He moved her when she didn't want to be moved. Inexplicably Beck didn't resist. Safra spoke to Harvey in a condescending tone.

"Harvey, get Ms. Oldman, Rebekkah, and me a drink. Sparkling water with lemon, or would you prefer a beer? No, that's right, you enjoy beer alone, when watching an old Bulls' game, or with tacos, or after sex. So sorry the last activity has been so absent in your life. Two waters, Harvey."

Harvey was shocked. How the hell did Safra know those things about Beck, were they even true? He tried to make eye contact with Beck but Safra kept a tight grip on her shoulder. It was if he had stunned her into submission. She felt fury and repulsion but could not act on it. She wanted to sit in a chair but she didn't struggle when he seated her on the sofa and sat very close to her.

"Beck, I am very sorry to hear about the death of Jasmine Gordon. The death of any child is a tragedy. I feel the sorrow this has caused you, the pain."

Harvey returned quickly with the drinks. He sat next to Beck. He felt a sudden pang of protectiveness for her. There was something ominous in the way Safra interacted with Beck. Regardless, Harvey didn't drop a bit of his obsequious behavior. "Me too, Beck, all that Richard said, exactly."

Harvey's meaningless sentiment helped her regain herself. "Oh, really, you feel so much. Tell me exactly what it is you feel, Harvey." Before he could speak, Safra took over again. "Harvey, I believe you were going to check the leads that have come in, you know the reward." Beck knew Harvey. She knew what a proud, tough cop he had been. She could not believe that he allowed Safra to belittle him, and especially in front of her. Harvey was ordered out of his own office again.

"Beck, don't leave until I have a word with you." Harvey left but his disgust remained.

Safra situated himself to look at Beck directly. "Excellent. Most people do not so much as glance at me, let alone stare. Fear of looking into the Devil's eyes."

"Devil. Isn't that a trifle self-aggrandizing? No, I wasn't staring. I was trying to find that pain you feel so deeply," she said coolly.

"And, did you?" he asked blandly.

"Why did you throw Harvey out of his own office, Mr. Safra? What do you want from me?"

"I want your passion. I want that screw the rules attitude and energy I saw in the courtroom and just now when you spoke about Jasmine. I want you to harness all that I see and transfer it to my case."

"You're mistaken, what you see Mr. Safra, is abject failure."

"On the contrary, I see the birth of a lioness out for revenge for the killing of a cub. You and I share many of the same qualities in pursuing what we want. Make working for me one of your obsessions."

Beck jerked slightly. "What do you mean one of my obsessions?"

Safra smiled. "Please, call me Richard."

Beck drained the glass of water. "You heard me. I quit. I blew it. I caused my client to be murdered because of that stunt on TV. When I was a prosecutor I got to exact that revenge you referred to. Putting the scum in prison didn't make things whole, but it closed the circle. I can't do that as an investigator."

"Going on TV did not cause Jasmine's murder. There's a madman out there hunting. As to being a prosecutor, though you were a magnificent at it, you didn't always close the circle. Cases were lost, the LeMond case for a sorry example. I know what that did to you. Harvey convinced you to work by holding out the hope that you could vindicate yourself if you saved Jasmine. You still can find redemption. There is another person who needs your help."

Beck got up, stood in front of him. "So compassionate, who knew. I mean your connections, excuse me, your alleged connections belie compassion. To be, allegedly, aligned with criminal enterprises, corruption, arms dealing, not exactly things that make one think of compassion. Then there are the interesting tales of what happens to people who cross you." She made a face of fear, sucked in breath through her teeth.

"All fiction, but if you're concerned, don't cross me," he answered smoothly.

"If I worked on your daughter's case, I would go where the information leads me, even if it took me to your front door, Richard," she rejoined unequivocally.

Safra stood so his shoe was literally toe to toe with her moccasin. "Exactly the answer I had hoped to hear. Are we in business?"

"You pay for all the expenses that I incur investigating not only your daughter's disappearance but the investigation of Jasmine and Camille's murder until I say I'm done. That's one stipulation. The other is I don't like being spied on. I don't like your knowing what I drink or eat or who or when I fuck. Do not invade my privacy."

Safra's eyes narrowed, coldness replaced the feigned warmth.

"Privacy is an obsolete concept in this electronic society. Technology and a lazy, complacent population have taken care of that. I own one of the largest tech and media companies in the world. I have and will use it to my advantage." He took Beck's hands, held them in a vice grip.

"I am handing you a lot of power. I will know everything I need to know about you to be sure that I have not made a mistake. If that means some of your idiosyncrasies are known by me, so be it. Now, you look tired, it has been a hellish day. Go home, and don't worry about talking with Harvey. I'll take care of him."

He let go of her like a fisherman releases a fish off a hook. Once back in the water it leaves a wake of blood flowing from its ripped mouth and gills.

Beck was relieved that he no longer physically held her but she was like the fish, ripped up. She couldn't tell him to fuck off and that she was not going to work for him even though she had every intention to. She left the office. No one was in the reception area. She looked back in Harvey's office, no sign of Safra. No one. Beck began to wonder if she was awake. If only Pitt would show up. God, Pitt, she would love to see her. She would hug her with joy. Someone, some human being was needed to take the stain of Safra away. She needed an antidote for the poison that just infected her. The next thing she knew, she was at the elevator incessantly pushing the button to get the hell out of there.

***

It was three in the morning. The pounding on the door was ominous. Beck stood ready with a baseball bat, armed with fury. Bludgeoning would be a welcome release. She looked through the peephole. The tension drained from her body. She hid the bat in the closet.

"This better be earth shattering." She left him standing in the hallway as she went to the kitchen. Will made his way to the living room. To say he was shocked at the chaos and the unopened boxes would be an understatement. He began to understand at the very least that Beck was a supremely complicated person. She joined him dressed in her stained bathrobe, red moccasins, and in no better temper.

"What may I ask, Beck, do you need with three chainsaws?"

"I am starring in a horror film. What may I ask are you doing here at three in the morning?"

Beck threw clothes and garbage off the sofa to sit but only cleared a spot for herself. Will watched her throw things on the floor so he did the same. He had never seen a woman's apartment look like as bad as a man's, or even a frat house for that matter. "Geez, this makes my room when I was a teenager look…" He caught the narrowing of her blood shot eyes. He knew to change the topic and the tenor.

"I'm sorry it's so late, but I knew you wanted to know about Jasmine. The scene was very much like the one in the park. Her hands and genitals were mutilated. Emily was right about things seeming rushed, not so precise, even the cutting. Her neck was broken, that is the official cause of death."

"I'm getting a beer," she paused, "beer, you want one?" He nodded.

Beck returned quickly with two opened bottles. Will took the bottle, looked at it.

"What? You need a glass?" she asked irked.

"Glass, what's a glass?" he asked.

"So detective, what does all of this mean? Obviously there is some kind of ritual going on here. But what is its meaning? How does it help us find the killer?" Before he could answer she said, "I met Safra today."

Will choked on his beer. "You what? Why would you be in the same room with him? I hope you showered."

"A shower's not enough. He's going to pay and pay big for the investigations into the murders."

Will shifted uncomfortably. "These are homicides now and Camille's family never hired you, Beck."

"The police didn't do shit to find either girl, Will. I can help and work in ways that you can't."

"Beck, you were in the system, you know how it works, the politics."

"What are you saying? That you're not going to work with me because of Safra's money? Or now that Jasmine's dead, I should give up and do what? I'm not out of this and time is running out for Tamara."

Will picked up the VHS box titled Bulls. "You're a Jordan fan," he assumed.

"No, yes, but it was Rodman who got me into the Bulls. I related to the way he alienated everyone but always got the job done. Underneath the wild hair and the wedding dress is someone who had to slug his way through life. No easy doors opened for him. For any outcast he was a true role model. When I feel wiped out I watch the old Dennis be a champion,. I like people who bend rules that were stacked against them from the word go." Beck realized she revealed too much. She shifted uncomfortably.

"Blake wrote that it is the way of a child to never enter the world of the censor, miniature anarchists. A poet's way of saying that people who aren't tied down by what others think and don't follow the rules will exact penalties for being an individual."

"Gee, Will, exactly who are you talking about?" asked Beck.

"I include myself." Will got up and stretched. "You look like shit, partner. I'll see you tomorrow." He kissed Beck on the cheek. After he closed the door, Beck began to clear off the coffee table.

***

Beck tried three times before she got the guts to knock on Miles Gordon's door. The minute he appeared, she knew she might not do what she needed to. The police gave him the devastating news about his daughter, searched his home, and left him in ruins. Miles didn't drink or do drugs, but the agony became too much and on the day his daughter's body was found he saturated his brain with alcohol. He couldn't fully comprehend what they said or what happened even when he went to the morgue and identified his little girl's lifeless body. Beck could not look into his eyes when she spoke. She was afraid of his pain, afraid of his righteous incrimination.

"I have no excuses; you have no reason to believe me, but I will find the son of a bitch." She promised.

Miles motioned for Beck to enter his home. He went to another room, returned with Jasmine's Rodman jersey.

"You got something to say to me?" he asked. Beck looked straight into his eyes. "Jasmine knew about her mother. She kept that from you. I did too. I should've told you as soon as I found out. Even though you feel betrayed by me, I want you to help me. Ask around about this so-called friend who told her about Dianna. Look again, as my friend would say with fresh eyes." Miles spoke very slowly.

"Did that with you, looked at you with fresh eyes. Heard you were a helluva fighter in the courtroom. You keep this jersey of Jas's. She had her hands full trying to defend 91. She's…she was a fighter, like you. You were hit before and I know you're down again. Tough shit. Get over it, be the old you and get him."

Beck reached for the jersey, but what she got was all of Miles' weight and grief as he embraced her small frame and sobbed. Beck's arms couldn't reach around him, but he felt as if he were hugged by ten very strong people.

Ten

The fluorescent lights in the murder room colored everyone a sickly green. The filthy windows sweated from the heat outside and inside. A few utilitarian steel chairs were scattered about the room. A whiteboard on wheels squealed as it was pushed to the front of the room.

Crime scene photos were taped near the names of Jasmine, Tamara and Camille. Olivia Safra's name was separated from theirs. Will, Jim, with other detectives waited quietly. An older, balding Lieutenant stood at a podium.

"See that board? What's up there is known as a cluster fuck. Two girls have been found, murdered, mutilated. Two too many. On top of that, one girl is still missing, Tamara Hughes. And do I even need to mention the S word? Safra's been gone for weeks. If her father were more precise, we would know exactly when he noticed she was not in his life. If all of that is not enough, thanks to our young TV star, the African American community is really pissed off, and so is the mayor." An audible groan of anger and agreement accompanied this assessment. "By now they'd be pissed anyway and with damn good reason. So, Blake, get your ass up here, tell us what we should know."

Will moved to the podium. His glossy hair, cobalt eyes, rock and roll T-shirt irritated every molecule in every detective in the room. They never fully accepted him. He was always that rich Ivy League kid playing at being a cop. Will knew this and couldn't blame them. "We have nothing. I mean nothing. Not a hair, finger print, sighting, witness, nothing. There must be a safe house where he's isolated and can take his time to go through all of the rituals. This is a well-planned enterprise. The cutting is exact, not surgical, but carefully done and time consuming. He bathes them, brushes their teeth, shampoo's their hair. He had to shop for underwear. Shop for the dolls, stuffed animals, fake flowers. These girls are not any girl. They are of the same race, gender, age, from the same geographical area. The offerings, as we call them, are placed in a particular fashion There is no evidence that these are sex crimes. There are no signs of struggle or ligature wounds to show they were bound. It leads me to the conclusion that the victims were lured, or they went willingly. Maybe he is a known person to the girls, or uses the old ploy of a puppy or your parent is hurt. He is doing something to gain their confidence so they will go with him, quietly. We have background checks going on for teachers, anyone who works in their school district, store owners, street vendors, the guy who sells ice cream out of the truck, if that still happens."

"What is the significance of the items at the scenes?" asked the Lieutenant.

"The fact that all of these things, flowers, candles, toys are white is important. White is the color of purity, innocence, and in some cultures death. The lamb can be a religious symbol of Jesus. The baby dolls may mean childhood. Then again, white artifacts placed by murdered African Americans may be connected to White Supremacy."

"And Olivia Safra?" a detective asked. The Lieutenant joined Will at the podium. "I think we can agree that the only thing the Safra case has in common is that she is a missing person. She is older, wealthy, though half black, that is not enough of a similarity. Plus, there are lots of motives for taking a rich, powerful man's kid. The motive as to the taking and killing of these girls is what?" A murmur of consensus followed.

"There is one other thing in common. No one has ever come forward with a demand or ransom for any of them."

"Safra is a spoiled rich kid. She could be pissed at her father, jet setting anywhere on this planet," Jim said with contempt. "Who knows if she is missing or just left causing us a big fat pain in the ass." There was a lot of agreement with Jim's comment.

"Okay. No forensics and no leads is bullshit. There is no mastermind out there; we just haven't found his fuck up. We're missing something beyond what we know that connects these girls. We're looking, but not seeing. You know the drill. The profile is a youngish white male, twenties to forties, but don't leave the older guys out. This is the guy everyone doesn't notice and once identified is always the quiet, never caused a day of a trouble blah blah. Start searching the files for priors who committed crimes against African Americans, rapes, use of knives, affiliation with hate groups. Check the neighborhoods. See who has not gone to work, missed school. Burn up your phones and shoe leather."

Will couldn't believe that the Lieutenant said looking but not seeing, maybe there was hope for him. Maybe he was a closet reader of poetry.

"Blake, you deal with the Press. You're who they want to talk to but this time you do it from a department script. Oh, and Blake, you stay away from Oldman. She's bad news for us, literally."

Will nodded. He went to the back of the room, dialed his cell phone.

"Beck what are you doing tonight?"

***

Beck laid back on the headrest, carried away by the haunting music of Pink Floyd. Will looked over to the passenger seat of his Mustang, smiled. He turned down the music.

"You didn't need to do that. I can focus, just say it again." Beck sat up giving him her full attention.

"To know a miser you must see the beauty of a worn out wallet. That allows you to know what the miser values. So, we need to see with the eyes of the killer, try to see what it is he values in these girls from this area. He knows them. No screaming, no one reporting a kid struggling. The bodies show no evidence of being tied up. He's a normal presence in their lives. We have to see what he does."

"And by our cruising the projects, late at night, white people in a white teenager's car we're going to see like the killer?"

Will slammed on the brakes and jumped out of car. Beck was in a state of shock as she watched him run down into the dark street. She caught up to him just as he grabbed the arm of a screaming adolescent African American girl.

"Will, let go of her, now," she commanded. He obeyed. The girl stopped screaming. She looked for an escape route past the two white assailants. Beck spoke as calmly as she could. "It's okay. You're okay. He's a cop. Show her your shield. Goddammit, Will, show her," Beck ordered.

Will complied. He got the wherewithal to back away from the girl, give her some space. He was as freaked out as she was. Beck approached her but was careful not to crowd her.

"Hey, hey, are you okay?" The girl calmed but was not okay.

"How do I know that's a real badge? He doesn't look like a cop, and who the fuck are you?"

"All good questions, and an astute observation about him. You're very smart." Will and the girl just stared at Beck. "Jesus, Blake, talk to her."

"My name is Detective Blake. Will. She's Beck Oldman, a private detective." The girl looked at them in the dim light of the single working streetlight.

"Yeah, yeah, I think I saw you on TV," she said with some relief.

"What's your name?" Will asked regaining his calm.

"Ella, Ella King. I wasn't doing nuthin wrong, why are you after me?"

"Ella, like Ella Fitzgerald, I love her music."

Ella looked at Will, confused.

"He thinks everyone is named after a famous person because he is, ignore him. So, you said you saw us on TV, then you know it's not safe for you to be out here alone," Beck said in a nurturing tone that surprised Will.

Ella pulled out a canister of pepper spray from her purse. "My pop usually meets me at the bus stop, but he's real sick and can't. I don't get off work until midnight."

"Okay, maybe until he's well, you could take a few days off," Beck suggested.

Ella rolled her eyes. "Are you for real? Maybe you can take off from your white people's job, or is it your career, but if I don't show up to my job, my ass gets canned. My family needs every penny."

Will and Beck knew they were blowing it.

"Is there anyone who can meet you, any male friend, or relative?" Will pleaded. She nodded.

"Great, great. Listen, when you're out, day or night be very careful. Check out your space. Look inside parked cars, or cars that slow down next to you," Will spoke carefully. He wanted to get the points across without scaring the shit out of her.

"And be really careful when some crazy person runs after you. You did exactly what you should have tonight," Beck quipped.

"Except you caught me," Ella rejoined.

"Okay, you're right, so next time, you have that pepper spray out." Will was disturbed by her astute comment. Was this the way the killer got the girls? Said he was a cop. Beck was ahead of him in thought.

"Ella, anyone chases you, run until you have no legs left." Now they did it. They scared the shit out of a teenager just trying to go home after slopping out greasy fries for eight hours and minimum wage.

"We're going to take you home; my car is around the corner," Will commanded.

"What he means is we will walk you to your door, right Detective. Not have you get in a car, right?"

Will nodded. God he thought, how much worse he could blow it. Ella walked in between them as they moved out of the light into the recesses of the projects. What they didn't notice, which was ironic since Will had admonished Ella to pay attention, was that their picture was being taken by a person in a parked car. A car that Will did not check out.

***

Pink Floyd was replaced by Miles Davis. Will drove very slow. The windshield wipers kept time like a metronome to Beck and Will's shallow breathing.

Beck spoke carefully. "Will, get control of yourself or you'll blow it and end up like me."

"I've been hoping you would tell me what happened with the Lemond case," he said gently.

Beck wiped the condensation from the passenger window. "That prick was raping his nine-year-old daughter. LeMond was the Mayor's right hand man, more like a bag man. When he finally got arrested there was immediate pressure from upstairs to dismiss the charges. I was so stupid, no naïve, a word I don't apply to myself. We had pictures, witnesses, the medical evidence. Open and shut. We waited for the Mayor to throw him under the bus."

"He had something on the Mayor," Will asserted.

"They had something on each other. There was intense pressure put on me to get the heat off of LeMond. Injustice and pressure, a destructive cocktail for me. I should have handed the case to another prosecutor because a meltdown was coming. I have a problem, okay I have lots of them. When I feel cornered or helpless, I shoplift." She waited for Will to respond.

"So what happened?" Will's tone was neutral.

"I didn't hand over the case. I told them that I was prosecuting that rapist to the full extent of the law and would be asking for maximums in sentencing. That just ignited their wrath. Each day I became less in control until I found myself walking out of a store with a three dollar bag of bolts stuffed in my pocket. It's like I go on automatic pilot, then I am shocked that I get away with it, but not this time. This time I was caught by LeMond's private police force made up of homicide and vice cops. They had been following me for weeks. I don't know if he knew that I shoplifted or was just hoping to catch me doing something."

"So what? Shit, that's nickel and dime stuff."

"Will, it's a moral turpitude crime. You know that. If I had six pounds of coke it would have been better; addiction is an illness. Stealing is ignoring the difference between right and wrong. Plus the Mayor wanted to burn me, so it didn't matter if I took a pack of gum. He threatened to put the story out, with pictures. Try me in the Press, get me disbarred. He even dangled the threat of jail. He said he could use me as an example to show his no tolerance for corrupt officials. He was going to burn me down to protect LeMond, a pedophile, just a day of politics in the city."

Will started to turn off the music. She stopped him. "I love Miles Davis."

He left the music on. "You said you shoplift. That denotes a pattern."

"The first time was when I was ten-years-old. I had been home alone for over a week. My mother was never there. She fell apart when my father took off, and then her sister was diagnosed with schizophrenia. She had me too young. No money, no family. It was overwhelming, and she was a weak person. To handle it she would disappear. Right before she took off she would stock the house with junk food, and to her credit she came back when I was down to my last candy bar. I would get myself to school, but I was dirty, smelled. The water and power were shut off a lot. I had to learn how to make myself invisible so no one would ask questions. She used to threaten me with foster care and orphanages if I didn't toe the line. What Goddamned line? I never knew what she meant. Probably she meant I should not be there one of the times she came back, but I was. I ate leftover food from cafeteria trays, stuff out of the garbage. I handled it until this one time when she didn't come back. I was exhausted by the darkness and the fear. I hated it when she didn't pay the rent and the landlord pounded on the door. I was sick of the constant hunger but more than anything I loathed having no control. It finally built into rage. I ran to the store, swiped a box of cupcakes. I loved the adrenalin. The instant way my brain took over, plotted how to hide the box and not get caught. The control I had to have to walk slowly out the door. I owned myself. I put one over on the store clerks. My helplessness evaporated and euphoria took its place. I ate every one of those synthetic cakes until I puked my guts out. The pattern was set. If I felt out of control, I would shoplift. Those boxes you see in my apartment are me trying to get better. I've switched stealing to compulsive buying. That TV shopping has to be putting people into bankruptcy. I've been in and out of therapy forever."

"Me too, lots of years of being shrunk," Will sighed.

Beck looked at him sympathetically. "I know about your sister, Will, that she was murdered."

"She was murdered, then dumped by the side of the road. She was coming home from school when he got her. No one was ever caught. I was supposed to pick her up that day, but I was too into me, too fucking busy. I couldn't give my kid sister fifteen minutes? We live and die by instant choices. I will own that guilt until I'm dust. I try to navigate the world knowing what I did, trying to survive it. I have no room to judge others."

"You should judge me, I do. To get out of the shoplifting charge, keep it out of the news, and most important, not get disbarred; I agreed to throw the case by claiming the cops got the pictures from a dirty search. I burned really good cops. I even looked like an honest ADA admitting the case went wrong. I am nothing but fear and loathing to the force. The Mayor never planned to let me off the hook. He had to wipe out my credibility in case I ever changed my mind and came clean about myself and his blackmail. He released the story that I was behind the dirty search, manipulated the probable cause. He showed me the pathetic pictures of my stealing. I let him run the story that I was emotionally unstable, untrustworthy and lost an open and shut case because of my mental state. I put myself first, like what you said about what you did with your sister. Except the difference is Will, you weren't doing anything wrong. You were a kid. I chose my career, I chose me over that girl. My career was my life. I made it through law school to get the bastards and the scum, but in the end, I became scum."

Will parked the car. They listened to the last notes of Miles Davis. Will turned to Beck. He wanted her to pay close attention to him.

"A person is more than one mistake, even a huge one. Look over your life. It's amazing you survived that David Copperfield childhood. Your record is large on putting away dangerous bastards. You've saved lots of people from predators, and don't you dare tell me you're responsible for Jasmine. Beck, that's almost an egomaniacal thing to say. You're not responsible for some whacked out killer who's getting messages from dogs or God to kill girls. You're trying to stop him. You're a good guy."

Will had to breathe deeply, he was feeling anger, compassion, and frustration. He was dragged back into the pit of reliving his sister's death. Beck felt his anguish.

"Will, the point of this humiliating confession is that I see the self-destructive tendency in you that I have. This stunt with Ella tonight, chasing a black girl in the projects when a murderer is preying on black girls? Jesus. How out of control is that? The brotherhood in Blue is real. Those detectives will destroy you, worse, they'll help you destroy yourself. I can't let you be ruined because of some confused loyalty you feel for me. I'm not your sister, Will. You can't save her by saving me. You can only burn yourself."

Will looked at Beck, his eyes brimmed with tears. He kissed her, not like her brother.

Beck only slightly pushed back. "You didn't hear a word I said. You're just like me, that's so depressing." Beck got out of the car and didn't look back at Will.

***

Beck did not look like herself in the fitted clothes, perfect makeup and hair. Not a smear or moccasin to be seen. She was cool, serene, a marked contrast to Harvey's high wire tension revealing itself in a noticeable twitch of his eyebrow. Finally the massive oak doors of Richard Safra's mega estate opened.

They were escorted by a young Middle Eastern male to a sumptuous living room where they were greeted by the impeccable Safra. It did not go unnoticed by him that Beck was an attractive woman.

"Jamal, you may leave now. Rebekkah, I do prefer to call you Rebekkah if you do not mind, please take a seat. You too Harvey, sit." Beck stole a look at Harvey; he smiled profusely as he sat on Safra's canine command. She wondered if Harvey would sit up and beg if Safra told him to.

"May I get anyone coffee, tea, anything?"

"No, thank you Mr. Safra," said Beck.

"Richard, please, call me Richard. Straight to business, I like that."

Beck walked around the room; Harvey's eyebrow went into double-time twitching.

"We need to ditch the reward. They yield nothing but crack pots and crack heads," Beck said in a matter of fact tone.

Harvey held his finger to steady his brow. "We didn't agree on that, Beck."

"And we need a current picture of Olivia," she added.

Safra stood in the center of the massive room. "You and the police have the most current picture available."

Beck thought of Miles' apartment. The furniture could not accommodate all the pictures of Jasmine depicting the stages of her short life. There was not a single picture of Olivia in the museum-sized room. Only tasteful paintings that boasted of

Safra's wealth. The house was not a home, it was a gallery. A gallery glorifying the wealth and power of the man.

"But that picture was when she was a teenager. There must be a picture from the university, a driver's license. What about a passport?" Beck argued.

She confronted Safra. "How do you not have a picture of your daughter?" she demanded.

The heavy sigh mixed with a groan came from Harvey, who could barely hold his brow from jumping off of his face. Safra's stance became slightly wider, his eyes narrowed significantly, they deadened, slightly. He changed from a genial host to the embodiment of the person who haunts dreams.

Beck was undaunted. "And Olivia's mother? Come to think of it, I have never heard her mentioned, let alone seen her. Please tell me about her."

"Her mother has been dead for years. Our marriage ended after the birth. Her mother took her to her country, the Democratic Republic of Congo. Boarding school seemed the right approach after her mother's death. It wasn't until she entered college that she came to this country. I provided her with a lovely apartment. I also provided a room here but I don't believe she ever used it. She had the option to when I was away on business. Of course, if I had a son, things would have been different, very, very different." Safra's voice was a mix of anger and regret.

Harvey and Beck exchanged a fast look.

"How?" Beck asked.

"What?" Safra responded, still lost in the fantasy of having a son.

"How would things have been different if Olivia was a male?" Beck queried.

Harvey winced at what he was sure was the last straw for Safra. Instead of rage, Safra was calm, perhaps a rare moment of weakness.

"He would have lived with me. I would have had sole custody. He would have learned our religion, traveled the world, worked with me. Never would he have stayed in such a primitive country, with a woman as his mentor," his voice was laced with agony. Beck sucked in every syllable; she began to feel a metal taste of disgust in her mouth.

"So, you don't really know Olivia, do you?" she asked derisively.

Safra struggled to retain the dream of a son for just a few more seconds, but that woman robbed him of them. He couldn't let his voice betray the fury he felt toward her.

"I was pleased to find a bright, young woman who embraced the teachings of Islam," he answered pleasantly.

"You're Muslim?" Beck asked with shock; she hated her tone. It sounded as if she had a prejudice, what she had was fury that things were kept from her that made her look stupid. Things that might help find Olivia.

"Really Harvey, have you not briefed your employee? Is it your lack of professionalism, or is it hers? Did you not get a file from Wilder, and if not, do you not have the initiative to do even a cursory computer search on, a very high profile client?"

As Safra lectured her, Beck concentrated on his eyes. They were so light that at times he looked as if he were blind. His daughter's sable eyes, filled with life, and all he could do is wish she didn't exist. He wanted a replica of himself, of course he would. Thankfully the world didn't grant his wish. Her animosity toward him was stopped by a hissing sound that came from Safra.

"Yessss," he hissed, "Muslim. I was born in Jordan, as was my father and his father. My mother was American but her faith was the same. I was married in Africa to an African woman. She was a devout Muslim."

Beck took notes. She kept her eyes fixed on the paper while she spoke.

"The picture you're painting of Olivia is of a very sheltered, conservative, orthodox woman who was thrust upon the wilds of an American university in a large city. Did she find it hard to adjust to American culture? Here women are brought up to think of themselves as equals, not second to men in anyway. Sons are no more valued than daughters in this country."

That was it, Harvey's eyebrow twitches and heart palpitations were off the charts.

"Excuse me, Richard. Where is the bathroom? And I want to say, Islam, or is it Muslim, well it's my favorite religion."

Neither Safra nor Beck dignified Harvey's groveling. He left the room, as far as they were concerned he had never been there. Safra slowly addressed Beck's remarks

"She was brought up to be circumspect. Respectful to her betters, to know who her betters were and that there is honor in serving a father and eventually a husband. She was trained to be careful in her choices, to value her body. She learned to honor her family and not bring shame by indulging in acts that would make her a vessel for debasement. Shakespeare wrote, be true to thyself. That is what she was taught. Isn't that what a modern woman is striving to do? If so, then how could her teachings create, as you put it, problems adjusting?"

Beck nodded, wrote feverishly. Without looking at him she interrogated him.

"Does your daughter, does Olivia know that you are very disappointed that she is not a son?"

Safra's eyes watered. It was clear that he was not used to being questioned and never challenged by a woman. Control was his mantel. He checked himself. He had to be sure he did not display any weakness, or reveal the ills he suffered from her impudence. His voice was tight but clear.

"She received a first class education that cost hundreds of thousands of dollars and will continue in medical school. She has a very strong mind that doesn't crack under pressure."

He took the pad from Beck, made her look at him. He wanted to see her reaction; he hoped his last words antagonized her. Instead, she smiled, waited for him to continue. He couldn't know that when Beck felt in control, it was close to impossible to penetrate her veil. His words were not even an annoyance for her, on the other hand he had moved from annoyance to anger. He was not used to losing. He continued but had to move away from her, mostly to keep himself from lashing out. He dropped her pad on the table; he wanted her to have to pick it up. She did, gleefully.

"She adheres to her religion, faithfully, scrupulously. She believes that women are more than equal. Women who are equal do not sell themselves cheaply to hormone driven, brainless males whose futures will entail flipping burgers. So no, Rebekkah, she did not have trouble adjusting to the weak, debased culture of an

American campus. As to an American city, her level of sophistication was cultivated when she summered in Paris, Madrid, Cairo. American culture a problem, what an insult."

Beck wrote furiously. She watched as Safra moved deeper into the shadows of the cavernous room. The distance did nothing to dispel his seething. Beck knew she had to make amends.

"Mr. Safra, I know these are tough questions but I need to know about Olivia. Can you tell me about the last contact you had with her."

"Read the report," he sneered.

"I have. I need you to tell it to me. Maybe something will come to mind that didn't make it to the report."

Beck's impudence displayed in his home would be something he would have to address another time. Her refusal to call him Richard, a command not obeyed. She would be easy to get into line; her weaknesses were so easily triggered. Revenge was a dish he liked to serve ice cold.

"I know that she joined some student organization, and no, before you ask, I do not know which one, or when, or why. It lasted a moment, a dalliance."

"A dalliance, from such a serious minded woman? That's odd. Did something happen?" Beck re-engaged the battle.

The silence, as the saying goes, was deafening. Safra flipped cold contempt into an art form. Harvey returned to find the animosity in the room worse than when he left it. It was unbearable. He grabbed Beck's notepad from her hands and stuffed it his pocket. She was too shocked to punch him.

"Okay, I believe we have another appointment and have taken far too much of your time, Richard, let's go Beck."

"Mr. Safra, I..." Beck stammered as she resisted Harvey.

"Richard is what you've been told to call me," he seethed. Beck refused because he demanded it and because it got under his skin.

"Oh yes right. Um, I need to see Olivia's room. I know you don't know if she used it, but if she did, maybe something useful will turn up. If nothing else I could tell you if your daughter ever stayed in your house. Heck, maybe even dig up another photograph of her to add to your collection of the one."

Harvey grabbed Beck's elbow. "I said we're going now." Beck got up, finally. Safra was still processing Beck's sarcasm. She tried another tactic.

"If not here, today, then how about her apartment? Can we get the landlord to let us into her apartment?" Harvey could not get Beck to move. Safra realized he needed to shut her up. He went to a massive, shiny black desk that looked very much like a sarcophagus. The crypt motif had not been lost on Harvey. It added to his anxiety.

When Safra walked back to them, into the light, his anger was obvious. He had lost the battle of control. Beck noted it and involuntarily walked back as he approached her. Flight took over the fight instinct. He liked that; she hated it.

"I am her landlord. I own the building," he said imperiously.

He dropped a key into her hand, careful that skin did not touch skin. Then, like a wraith, he left the room. Harvey cramped every muscle as he made himself walk, not run out of Safra's house.

***

Beck slammed the Mercedes' door, twice. The first time did not annoy Harvey nearly as much as she wanted. She almost fell out of the speeding car when she opened the door to slam it again. Harvey peeled out of the Safra estate from zero to sixty. Beck scrunched down in the seat. She refused to look at Harvey as he sped down the tree-lined drive. As they exited through the stone-walled gate, they spoke at the same time.

"What fuck?" They stopped, irritated at the chorus. Harvey knew he better speak first or he was toast.

"Me? What the fuck? What the fuck you? You tried to piss him, off, you tried. What the fuck was that? "Are you…"

He stopped there. He knew the worst thing he could say to Beck was anything about her mental state. She knew he almost crossed the line.

"Too Goddamned bad, Harvey. We need to know about Olivia. How did I not know he was Muslim? And that crack he made about briefing me. Is it public knowledge? Is it even in his online profile? We need to know more about their relationship, her schooling. How are there no official pictures of her? She never got a driver's license, no current passport picture, no school ID photograph. Is this kid real? We need to know about his life. I know he's the reason she's gone. Maybe some asshole hated her because she's a devout Muslim. We need to check out that organization she joined. Did you know she joined a group? That she was a practicing Muslim? No, you didn't. Wow, great work."

"You had to insult him, to find out?" Harvey sped up each time he spoke to her.

"How? How did I insult him? He has a problem with women in general and specifically with his own daughter. Whining that Islam is your favorite religion. What does that even mean?" Beck slapped the dashboard instead of slugging Harvey. He knew he had to ratchet down his fear and anger.

"Beck, you…"

That's all she let him say. "Did you notice he never called her by name? Not one time did he say Olivia, always he referred to her and she. He didn't even say she was his daughter, did he? And that garbage about having a son would have been so different. That guy is the dictionary definition of misogynist." Her fury kept building. So did Harvey's evidenced by his doing seventy in a forty mile zone.

"You're going to blow this, Beck and then I'm going to have to kill you."

"Speaking of killing, have you told Safra that the chances of finding Olivia alive are practically nil?"

"No, because I want my chances of being killed by him to be nil. You know that you don't screw with this guy. You so much as blink funny at Richard Safra, you lose your eyelids."

Beck turned to Harvey, leaned on the passenger door. "So that's why you put me on the case, so it's my eyelids on the chopping block. Why did you take this case if you're so afraid of him?"

Harvey took his hand off the wheel, rubbed his fingers together, meaning money.

"Not if she's dead, Harvey."

"Beck, find the creep who killed her and serve him up on a silver platter to Safra. We'll never have to work again." Harvey reached over patted Beck's knee in a very awkward way.

"Oh, I see, we find the guy, give him to Safra to do what he wants which I'm sure will include some torture used by the Inquisition. No one will care since he owns the cops. We'll be rich and happy ever after. To think you were such a square cop. I can ignore what you propose because we're not going to find her or the creeps who killed her. This is not a random crime. Street thugs don't have access to people like Olivia Safra. There's no ransom, so what is it? Political, revenge? God, maybe some poor slob didn't know he grabbed Safra's kid? When he found out, he freaked. No, no, this is professional. Poking around to find answers is very dangerous, isn't it? What have you gotten us into, Harve? A guy who knows how to make people disappear, that's what." Beck escalated her tone with each awful possibility.

"Okay, okay, calm down. None of Safra's enemies have the cajones to take his daughter, whether he hates her or not because he's too—I heard about a guy who said something that offended Safra. His tongue was cut out, then a gun was held to his head to make him eat a tasty dish of tongue tartar." Harvey looked at Beck way too long for someone who was driving.

"Is that true, you son of a bitch?"

"What do we know, Beck? We know Olivia has no friends, not one can be found. Including Daddy. So, what's the deal? Why is he making such a big deal to find her, why not leave it to the cops? Because, because he has a reputation to maintain in society, and he wants the head of the guy who fucked with his property. He has to exact revenge, keep his cred in the world he occupies.

It's all about his reputation and nothing about fatherly love. If we can even provide a lead..."

When Harvey's phone rang; they both jumped. He answered, pissed that the phone scared him. "What did you want?"

Harvey handed it to Beck. "Why is my phone for you?" She ignored him, so he threw it in her lap. Reluctantly Beck spoke. "Hello? Oh, Will. Yes." Beck hung up. Her face drained of color.

Harvey glanced at her. "You got that hunted look, junior detective wants a date," Harvey smirked.

Beck took a full minute to respond. "Tamara Hughes' mutilated body was found."

Not a word was spoken on the ride back home.

****

Beck didn't turn the lights on in her apartment. She took comfort in the blinking red circle on the answering machine. It indicated the living had make contact with her. Answering machines, the perfect relationship. She could get the benefit of contact without expending any energy or emotion. She had enough death and people who disappeared from the planet. Beck didn't consider the message could continue the theme of the day when she pressed the button. She let out a breath of relief as she listened to her friend Mark. He spoke with the energy of the living. The truly living, not a sleepwalker like Beck.

"Hello Beck, its Mark Lennon. I'm pretty sure you're sitting there, listening, answer if the mood strikes. I'm in town for a conference, and I insist that I take you, Kate, and Janice out for dinner. Someplace with some swank, you know? Let's get dressed up. In my case that means clean underwear. God, how long has it been since we were all together? I'll call with the time and place, don't make up some bullshit. You're coming. Love ya. Bye."

He made her smile which slightly surprised her. Beck got a beer, kept the lights off. She often wandered in the dark. She got the remote for the stereo, flopped on the sofa, turned on Charlie Parker. His perfect trumpet began to take her away from Safra, Harvey, and Tamara. Oh Jesus, God, Tamara.

Just as Beck put her arm across her eyes, she thought she saw something move in the corner. She sat up, looked around. "Great, now I'm hallucinating," she said out loud.

Parker's trumpet lulled her into a place she wanted to live the rest of her years, but she only got seconds. She knew she hadn't hallucinated a sound. Something had moved. She stayed still.

She couldn't be sure if the breathing she heard was hers, so she stopped; nope, it wasn't hers. Beck knew all the shapes in the room, where things belonged; the darkness didn't subtract that knowledge. There was someone in there and he was coming toward her. Beck searched for the remote. She could see the figure move slowly her way. She barraged herself with silent orders. "Look asleep. Where the fuck is the remote? I need it now or it will be too late. I swear if I find it, I will be neater, God, I promise. God, who's God? Do you believe in God? What did I just feel?"

Beck managed to move her arm off the side of the sofa, she could touch the remote. "Sleeping people move when they sleep. Move, move your legs, dammit, move your legs. Now, pick it up, pick up the remote. How can this asshole think I fell asleep so fast, shut up, who cares, pick it up, NOW."

Beck sighed, clutched the remote. The figure stopped moving for what felt like hours. Then it lunged, right as Beck jacked up the volume to deafening levels. Drums and cymbals reverberated throughout the apartment. The figure fell to the ground, stumbled into a myriad of unopened boxes. Finally the door was ripped wide open and the dark form exited. Beck exhaled heavily. She turned off the stereo just in time to hear the jangle of the phone. Beck screamed her throat raw.

****

Every light blazed in Beck's apartment; she was on the floor, wedged into a corner of the kitchen. Someone pounded on the front door. She crawled on her hands and knees. Beck couldn't muster the guts to look out the peep hole. "Will?" she called.

"Yes, Beck, it's me."

She unlocked the three heavy steel bolts. Will embraced her. She allowed this for only a moment. "I'll get beer," she said weakly.

Will followed her to a small kitchen. The stainless steel stove looked as if it had never had been used. The refrigerator however was marred by fingerprints and smudges. Beck set a glass on a small oak table next to the beer. She leaned against the stove holding her bottle. Her hands were shaking.

"What happened, Beck? Was it a burglar? Anything taken?" Will tried to sound like a cop.

"No, no God, I'm sorry I called you so late," she apologized.

"You're sorry, sorry, come on. I don't see any forced entry. Nothing's disturbed, which is hard to tell here." He looked for her to smile a little. No dice. "What made him leave?"

Beck drained the bottle of beer before she answered. "Jazz. I listen to this particular CD constantly. I knew that the drums were coming in strong, lucky timing. I raised the volume and it scared him out. I don't think he was supposed to hurt me."

"Jesus, that was smart. What do you mean, supposed to?" asked Will.

"It was a professional break-in, sponsored by the rich and powerful Richard Safra."

Will stopped his beer in midair. "Safra? Why, you work for him?"

"Yeah, and he's unhappy at my lack of obedience. I've been sitting here thinking and nothing else makes sense. The guy would have hurt me, taken something. All he did was scare the shit out of me. This is Safra's subtle way to me know he is very unhappy with me. Only he could get his thugs in here. I'm a lockdown fanatic. I spent too many scary nights alone when I was a kid not to care about security."

Will looked around, nodded, "But you don't have an alarm system."

"No. I want to be secure, yes, but I want my privacy more. I don't want some company monitoring me." Finally the toll of everything seemed to be overtaking Beck. There was no color in her face; the dark circles under eyes looked purple.

"Beck, I know you're not okay, what can I do for you?"

"Will, do you like movies? she asked.

"Uh, yeah, yeah, I like movies," he answered mystified by the weird switch of topics.

"I love movies. One of my favorites is *Gloria*. Gena Rowlands; she's great. Gena, Gloria, gets stuck taking care of this mob guy's smart mouth little kid after the mob guy is murdered by another mob guy. The kid has a book that can put all of the bastards in prison. The problem for Gloria is that these wiseguys are her friends. She turns on them to help the kid. Now she's a target too. Tough stuff to take on the mob, protect a kid, and do it in high heels. Thing is she doesn't like kids, and neither do I, not really but I protected them through the law. Gloria did it by breaking the law. She was successful, but I blew it and I don't even wear high heels."

Beck knew she was rambling. She sat at the table, laid her head on her arms, and fell asleep. She sat up a few minutes later, no Will to be seen.

"Will? Will, are you still here? I have more beer." She hated the fear that found its way in her voice.

She got a knife from a wooden block, slowly walked through the apartment to her bedroom. He met at her at the threshold. Will hugged Beck. She didn't resist and let him lead her to the bathroom.

The water flowed from a faucet that looked like a small waterfall. The large tub filled with bubbles. A low intensity nightlight glowed. He slowly began to undress her.

"Will, Will, stop. I don't know how to do this, you know. I've been alone all of my life, just moments of company. And it doesn't make it easier that you are thirteen."

"I thought you told Kate I was twelve," he countered.

She shriveled that he had heard that remark. "Beck get in the tub, relax. I will be here so you can take time out from being Wonder Woman. If by any chance you want me…for anything, let me know. And so you know, by the way, years mean nothing to me when it comes to people. I'll go now because mature men have patience to wait for what they seek."

She turned off the water. Let her fingers glide along the bubbles. She took off her clothes, slipped into the water. It was more comfort than she experienced in a long time. Before she knew what she was doing, she called Will's name.

His appearance momentarily confused her. She was more confused when he didn't join her; instead, he got a small stool, sat next to the tub. He turned the water on, lifted the nozzle. She let her head fall back as he gently massaged her hair with shampoo. She never knew water to be so sensuous. When he guided the nozzle down her spine, she let out a soft moan that she hadn't heard or felt for a very long time.

"That's good Beck, relax."

He rinsed the last of the shampoo from her hair, wiped droplets from her eyes with his fingertips. Then Will undressed. She watched, her face was soft and open. She reached for him without an ounce of reserve.

***

Safra was reading when the man entered his study. He was a large man, dressed in black. He took off his beanie.

"Is it done?"

The man nodded.

"You were able to get all things taken care of, including the computer and she didn't see your face?"

Again the man nodded. Without looking up, Safra dismissed him with the wave of his hand.

***

Sun poured into the kitchen, burning away thoughts of intruders, murderers and cold hearted bastards who hated their own daughters, for a few precious moments. They sipped coffee, held hands. Will hated to break the spell. "Now that I have had a chance to really look around, I have to agree with you. This place is a fortress. Too bad you couldn't see his face," he said.

"I think if I had he would have had to do something to me. All I know is he's big."

"Do you have a gun?"

"No. If I had been near the kitchen or bathroom, then I would've been armed. My mother was a genius at using spoons, hair brushes, rubber hoses, all sorts of household items as weapons. Coat hangers are particularly useful. I have pepper spray and a baseball bat. I don't like guns. You're a cop. You know what goes wrong with armed to the teeth amateurs. All of that aside, the real reason I don't want a gun is because I wouldn't shoot once. I would empty the clip into the bastard."

Will agreed. He knew she wouldn't stop with one shot. Good idea, no gun for Beck. "Okay, Will, now you can tell me about Tamara. I'm okay."

Will spoke in his cop voice. "She was found in a cemetery, another second site. This time the guy left a stuffed lamb but no doll. Cause of death was a broken neck, and there's slight bruising to the body. That's new. It does seem things are not as orderly; some of the ritual is forgotten or rushed. But why? We don't know shit."

"That's not quite right," she countered. "We know he's leaving a message; someone is going to get it eventually. White that means what? Virginal, innocence, childhood, purity? And what about the burial sites. A park, a church, a cemetery. Nothing is degrading, places of respect, fun, family."

"All the girls are African American. Maybe the fact that all the objects are white may be signifying White Supremacy? It's where the Lieutenant has directed us to put our focus, hate groups, child molesters, especially anyone who is affiliated with any of those groups." Will didn't seem convinced. Neither was Beck. "No, Will, those groups hate. They're angry. Where's the anger? What in good standing Nazi skinhead is going to bathe them? They would dump the bodies in horrible places. They wouldn't show the respect, or dare I say the love that has been displayed. The killer is getting lucky if this is the focus of the cops. Why are they going this way?"

"Beck, murder and mayhem is hatred. Plus, just because they're racists, doesn't mean they're stupid. Maybe they are misleading us with phony rituals. That said, I'm with you. This is the focus because there's nothing else to explore. Everyone's beyond frustrated. Since I've been a detective, I've never seen anything…oh shit, I forgot. Miles Gordon called Harvey. He was looking for you. This was really early yesterday. Harvey didn't find out until after you got back from Safra's. Jasmine's mother died of an overdose. I found out at the same time I got the report on Tamara. I think Harvey was afraid to tell you, and to tell you that Miles is falling apart. So much happened yesterday."

Beck drank her coffee.

The awful news was fuel. She was going to find the killer, or die in the process. She wished the asshole who broke into her house last night would return. Maybe she should buy a gun after all.

Purified

Beck patted Will's hand to comfort him.

Eleven

Jesus, thought Beck, as she entered Olivia's apartment, another monument to Safra's wealth. This is the third frigid space she had to endure that was his domain. Beck wondered if monsters could actually live in a place called home, with all of the connotations that word brings to mind.

The two-story apartment was over five thousand square feet. There were little furnishing and no decorations. This was a place to store humans, not a place where humans lived. She dropped her bag down on the floor, swore she heard an echo. The one positive about the apartment was the very welcomed cool temperature. Outside it was one hundred degrees and one hundred percent humidity. Of course that didn't stop her from wearing jeans and a sweatshirt, but that was tied around her waist. Beck's sleeveless T-shirt was damp. She took out a pad and pen, and the damn phone.

"Now, the heiress. Is she an heiress? Should check Safra's will," Beck said out loud. "Where is this possible heiress to a tech fortune? Tech?" Where is it? Beck looked for a phone or a computer. There wasn't even a TV. There was an answering machine, an antiquated one like Beck's. The phone was gone, and so was the tape in the machine. Beck went into the kitchen. The refrigerator was barren, as were the cupboards. No dishes of any kind. On the counter was a stack of paper plates and cups. Beck thought that compared to Olivia Safra she lived like a party animal. She felt sorry for the poor rich girl.

Upstairs there were three unfurnished bedrooms, each with its own terrace and bathroom. As Beck rounded the corner to the master suite bedroom, something caught her eye. She dropped to the ground. Someone was in the room. Slowly she made her way to the threshold, stood to the side. No movement, no sound. She swung the door wide open. On the tall wall above the headboard hung a black Hijab and a long black gown, the traditional dress of Muslim women. She was relieved momentarily. Was the clothing hung in an effigy? Or was it hung to be worshipped? Why was it hung at all? Beck dug out the phone from her pocket. She had to remember not to let Harvey know she was grateful he made her use it or that he taught her how to take pictures with it. She took several shots of the wall.

Beck looked in the closet, a few black skirts, white shirts and another gown and veil. In the bathroom she found a used toothpaste tube, a bar of soap. Not a trace of lotions and potions that cluttered every woman's bathroom.

Beck slowly made her way downstairs. She noticed a small desk tucked far in a corner of the mammoth room. She took a wireless mouse from one of the drawers. She did one more sweep of the room, checked under the cushions of an armchair. The sofa was the kind that didn't have cushions. It was hard and stiff like the room. Beck sat, hunched over her notepad, lost in thought until a chill went through her body. Beck reached for her bag. This time this guy was going to get a mega dose of pepper spray. Then a hand slithered onto her shoulder, followed by a hot breath on her neck.

"Rebekkah, I am so glad I didn't miss you," said Safra. Beck's shiver remained, as did her hand in the bag.

"How did you know I was here? Are you having me followed?" Safra moved from behind her. He saw her moving her hand quickly from the bag.

"Rebekkah, so suspicious. I own this building, remember? The manager knows to notify me if anyone comes to this apartment. There, now you may disarm your, what is it mace or pepper spray?"

"My suspicious nature is one of my best traits." Beck put the notepad into the bag.

"I suppose you know another child was found. She was savaged and no one is one inch closer into finding this animal. The professionals are losing. I am losing faith in them."

"There's no connection to those girls and Olivia," said Beck in a mollifying tone.

Safra put his hands in pockets. "Is that supposed to make me feel better?" he bit back.

"Did Olivia live here? There's nothing here to show she did, or anybody really. I mean a few clothes, but no makeup, shampoo."

"Those are items of vanity, Rebekkah."

"Washing your hair is vain? Okay, then how about no computer or phone. There's an answering machine but no tape." She made up her mind to let him mention the Hijab and gown.

Safra adjusted his impeccable tie that lay perfectly against his silk shirt. Beck noticed the fineness of his garments. She also noticed he didn't have a bead of sweat on him, but then she thought because snakes don't sweat.

"No mystery. I had them removed," he answered imperiously.

Beck jumped up. "You did what? Don't you know there may be valuable information that the police could have used? Might give the professionals better odds if people didn't tamper with evidence."

It was back, the dead eye of a shark or the deadly eye of a Mamba, like Janice called him.

"Tamper. That is a loaded word, legal too isn't it, lawyer? There was no evidence, nothing of any use on the computer or any other item. I own the technology, the equipment used to examine computer hard drives. My companies wrote the forensic software. We monitor and create the surveillance programs used by forensic teams. My people train the forensic technicians."

"Yeah, but you aren't the one who should decide if an email she wrote about going to a movie or a crush on a guy is useful or not. Oh, I know, movies are shallow and she had no awareness of the sex."

Safra took his hands from his pockets. It awed him that Beck challenged him continuously. He admired her in spite of himself. This didn't detract from the anger it generated as well.

"I will send her computer, everything to Wilder. I want some progress on this. I can make you rich."

Beck began to gather her things. "Money is Harvey's thing, talk to him."

He walked to the sofa. His tone became conspiratorial. "I can pay you, Rebekkah, with revenge. It is worth a lot to take revenge against shall we theorize, a freed but guilty child molester, and against the petty ante politician who assured his freedom. Psychic rewards are powerful. I can pay you in many different ways. We are a team now."

Beck was stunned at the blatant offer to do damage to LeMond, but not so much she couldn't ask him what she had been dying to since she met him. "Find who? Who do you want me to find? You need to say it to me, or I quit."

For the first time his eyes had a darkness about them. His face flushed. She had pushed him too far. "Olivia," he hissed. When he spoke his daughter's name, Beck knew it came with a price she would have to pay.

He started to leave, as he went by her he touched her back. Beck's body went cold. Why did he touch her? Just to show his power? She waited several minutes before she looked out the window to see his limo and bodyguards waiting on the street. Safra appeared, as he started to enter the car, he stopped. He took a step back, moved to face the window but didn't, he just stood there. He knew she was watching; he controlled her. Beck couldn't get warm for the rest of that scorching hot day.

***

Beck walked up and down the aisles of the grocery store. She had legitimate business there. She was out of beer and coffee. She needed some decent food since Will came by and he ate like a normal person. She was shopping but that was not all she was doing. She felt, what she felt. Safra was crowding her. For every move she made in his direction he made ten more in hers, impeding her. There was something she was missing. She couldn't put the pieces together about his hiring her and the way he interacted with her. Her demons were getting stronger and they forced her to go down the cosmetics aisle to steal.

Beck put the food basket down, took out her wallet with the same hand that held a lipstick she took from the shelf. She pretended to look at the number of bills she had, even held up the ten and five, just in case the clerks were watching her. When she put the bills back into the wallet, she managed to slip the lipstick in with the money. She perused more items, and then went back to the drink aisle. She picked up a six pack, changed her mind put the beer back on the shelf and slowly exited the store. The theft did its job. It removed her fear and made her feel in control for a few precious moments, very few. The crash of guilt and self-recrimination came on quickly. Beck walked to a bus stop. She looked at her spoils. What an ugly shade. She rolled the lipstick up too far, it broke in half. She shoved the top on the broken stick, marring the silver tube with smears and hunks of the hideous pink color. Beck threw it in the trash. She wished she could throw herself in too. Instead, she started for home.

***

Beck was uncharacteristically curt with Ann. Ann was the opposite of Pitt. She was a secretary who had no other illusions other than she was a secretary who scored a really high paying job. She liked Beck. Ann seemed to get her, never noticed the stains on Beck's sweatshirts or the fact that the stains were on sweatshirts in the hellish heat.

"What the hell do you mean that I can't get the files on Richard Safra? I'm the lead investigator on the case."

"His files are encrypted and they are on Harvey's computer. He is the only who can access Safra's information," Ann said apologetically.

"Are you telling me there is no backup? No hard copies? What if the computer crashes? They do crash you know, in fact they crash the second you need them not to crash."

"We do have backup, all kinds including hard copies of key docs. We do except for, you know, Safra," Ann replied.

"Holy shit." Beck realized she was railing at the wrong person. She patted Ann on the shoulder, went into her office to rail at the right person, Harvey.

She turned on her computer. The pictures of the gown and veil hanging on the wall came out well and looked creepier in a picture than it did in person. She checked to see if Harvey responded to the email she had attached to the pictures. Nothing.

Beck dialed the desk phone.

"Harvey? What? Yeah, I am actually calling from my office and I am actually unable to access the files on Richard Safra. MY CLIENT. I need to see all of his holdings, his whereabouts when his daughter disappeared. I hope you got a copy of his will. You know the usual information an investigation compiles. He has Olivia's computer. Did you know that Harvey? Harvey, are you listening to me? HARVEY?"

Beck slammed the receiver about six times before she flipped it off and exited the office.

****

Beck loved the neighborhood near the university campus. The old brownstone buildings, the cafes, buckled sidewalks, diverse people. She loved the trees the most. The magnificent trees whose limbs created a vaulted, green cathedral above the cracked streets. She used to go the nearby parks to study her law books, eat a cheese sandwich, and revel in the fact that she was doing what she was doing. Before her mother died, Beck had made a kind of peace, or détente with her. They had little contact but when they did meet, it was on one of those days Beck studied in a park. Beck didn't hate her mother; she feared she would become like her. Afraid she would inherit her mother's mental instability as well as her aunt's. Beck had problems, but she was not schizophrenic and at her age, she was safe from that hell. She had tracked her life so kids were never an option. She didn't want even the potential to do to a child what was done to her. Beck plotted in those early salad days of law school to become a prosecutor so she could wreak havoc and destruction on anyone who abused a woman or a child. She found health and a life in law. It saved her from mental institutions and heavy drugs that gave a modicum of relief from a spiraling mind. It was that fear, to lose all of that, including her sanity that drove her to the awful darkness of the LeMond debacle.

Beck sat on a bench she had shared with her mother. It was situated under a huge tree that provided much needed shade. She noticed the student population consisted of many students from Asia and the Middle-East. The area was truly cosmopolitan. She realized English was not the dominant language spoken by those who passed by.

The thunder rolled through the park. More rain to come, more lightning strikes. The lightning had been particularly harsh that summer. Splitting trees and causing fires. People loved summer because winters were so brutal, but this summer was different. This summer had people wishing for autumn. A thin Middle Eastern man approached her. He stopped and faced her directly.

"Hi, are you James Ibish? I'm Rebekkah Oldman, Beck."

Beck got up to shake hands, but he pretended not to notice. He was going to be fun, thought the very weary Beck.

"My name is Mustafah. James is my American name. I go by the name of my grandfather," he said disdainfully.

"Oh, wait, aren't you an American?"

He shook his head, irritated. "Only by birth."

That caught Beck off guard. "Oh, only by birth. Well, don't worry that barely makes you an American." Beck sat back down. She talked herself out of laughing at this young man's ludicrous attitude. He looked at her with a clear touch of hatred.

"Thanks for coming Mustafah. I won't keep you long. I know these summer sessions are intense. I was told that you knew Olivia Safra."

He looked around, checked out people who walked by. He was nervous.

"Do you feel uncomfortable talking here? You said not to meet at the university."

He shook his head but continued to look around, never at Beck directly.

"Are you a medical student?" she asked.

"No."

"Then how did you meet Olivia?"

"We met at political student alliance meeting. It was for Islamic students, or students interested in learning about Islam. The females had no business there. Politics is a man's domain," he said imperiously.

Beck tried to ignore his remark but she couldn't stop herself. "Oh, no females. So that's why politics and the world sucks."

"In the country of our grandfathers, women cannot speak to men the way they do here," he said lividly.

"And that's why, sonny, your mother lives in the United States." She thought he was about to burst a blood vessel.

"That's it. I am done with you." He stomped off.

Beck tried to control her laughter when she realized he was about to get away from her. She had to run after him. "Come on Jimmy, oh shit, I mean Mustafah. Mustafah. Please, I'm sorry, really. Olivia Safra is missing, you know that. I'm convinced something horrid has happened to her. You've read the papers. You know about the murders. Please, tell me, did Olivia agree with you about the role of women? Anything you can share could be very helpful." He refused to make eye contact with her. He behaved a lot like Richard Safra. "She agreed that women in western culture are debased." Just as he spoke a bus went by, bearing an ad for women's underwear. The model was dressed in a bra. The underwire made her breasts into a double Mt. Everest. The look on her face was inviting someone to make "the climb." Mustafah turned his look of disgust directly toward Beck. "She was sickened by what we just witnessed. She could not stomach the suggestive clothing, easy sex talk, music lyrics, everything in this culture. She said it was the cause of abuse and the demeaning of women and children."

"Did you notice that she became, I dunno, maybe more upset by these things? Did she change any of her behavior?" Beck asked.

"She began to wear the Hijab and the black gown. Not always. She said she wore it on days she needed to be protected."

"Protected? From what?" Beck asked.

Mustafah again turned his gaze directly to Beck. "Protected from women like you." Beck almost felt like she had been slapped. It took her a moment to recover. He enjoyed her reaction.

"This is, shall we say, a controversial stance; especially on college campus where many young women may disagree, strongly. Did she make enemies with this attitude?" she countered.

"I don't know about that. I do know she was difficult to be around. She was withdrawn, sullen. Of course there is the taint of her father. The stories of his dealings in the world, like selling arms to the highest bidder didn't sit well with many students. There is always resentment against the offspring of powerful people. She never spoke of him around me. I don't have any answers. I can only tell my impression and that is she was extremely unhappy. Now, I am done speaking with you."

Beck watched until he was out of sight. She worked on her notes. She looked up like people do when searching for the right word. She didn't find the word but she did find Jamal, the man who answered the door at Safra's estate. He stood across the street, blatantly watching her. Beck dialed her phone. "Hey Kate, are we on? Okay, I will meet you guys at eight. Yeah, it will be great to see Mark. Please shut up about Will, bye." She looked down only for the moment it takes to turn off a phone. When she looked across the street, Jamal was gone.

****

The parks in the city were as crowded as ever. The murders and missing girls did nothing to deter the crowds especially of poorer people. They didn't have air conditioning, or summer homes with private pools, or even fresh fruit. No, their only respite from the heat, humidity, and the peeling paint on the walls were the parks. Since the parks were so crowded people believed they were a safe place for kids. So the baseball games, barbecues, make out sessions, drug deals, and gun deals went on without a hitch.

Tillson Park was the prime spot for the latter of aforementioned activities. It was right in the middle of a housing project. There was no lush green lawns, tennis courts, slides, or a sandbox, which may have been a good thing. Even the swings were broken. It did have a baseball diamond and some rusted barbecues. It also had the reputation of a being a very dangerous place. This left the park to a multitude of illicit congregations. Amen.

The black sedan slowed down. Reflected on the windows was the baseball game played in the distance, and the face of a pretty girl, alone at a picnic table. She noticed the car; it was the third time it past her. She got up, watched it round the corner. On its next pass, only the game and an abandoned picnic table were reflected on the glass.

Twelve

The wait staff was dressed in black tie, vests, and was superb in its service. Sparkling chandeliers hung from a beautifully painted ceiling. Linen, silver, and the finest china adorned each table. Beck, Janice, Kate, and Mark, a heavy set, semi balding man held up champagne flutes. The women were resplendent in the candlelight. Beck even managed a smile, a real one.

"A toast to all the women at this table. Women I loved and was rejected by. Bitches, every last one of you."

They clinked glasses and drank heartily. "Oh, now Mark, honey, you were too busy saving the world to be chasing us," laughed Kate.

"What I remember is that you dear Kate were busy chasing fame and money."

"Well, that didn't work out," she said, without laughing.

"Mark," moaned Kate. "How is it that not one of us has ever been married?"

Janice leaned in, as if she were telling a secret. "Because we aren't capable of committing to having breakfast, let alone a relationship."

Kate shot a sly look Beck's way. "Well maybe that's about to change or at least Beck here might be able to commit to a junior meal." Fire could have turned to ice with the look Beck sent Kate's way.

"Oh, do tell," demanded Janice.

"Mark," said Beck, "tell us about Africa."

"Not a chance, Beck. Kate, do tell." He said slyly.

"Well the really romantic part, if you were Beck that is, their dates consist of tracking down a serial killer."

"Oh no, you mean that detective that was on your show?" asked Janet.

"Wait, I know I have been gone, but Beck, you're working? I thought you were, um, you know." Mark asked, carefully.

"I finagled a PI license, not practicing law. I got a case a missing person case, a young girl who was found murdered. Her case is connected to the others, Mark. I'm surprised you don't know about this." Beck was disturbed that she could rattle through the ashes of her life like it was a grocery list.

"Yes, yes, I know some," he said, "I've been so busy with meetings. Today was really my first day with some time off. Is this connected to Olivia Safra?"

"Beck's working that case too," added Kate.

Mark put down his glass, scrutinized his friend Beck. "I do know that young girls were murdered and their bodies mutilated. The mutilation aspect is fascinating."

"Mutilation is fascinating." Janice repeated with disgust.

"No, not like you make it sound. I mean, how and where they were cut is. Okay, I am going to start again. How were they cut?"

"Not surgically, but skillfully. I think that's what you mean," said Beck.

"That's it. Kate, you need to use the bathroom," demanded Janice. Kate did not need to use the bathroom. She didn't want to leave but followed the code of women: no woman goes alone with her gossip to the ladies room.

"You know Mark, Beck's always been a lousy influence on you. When we come back, we only talk about people who are not cut into pieces," Janice said curtly.

"She's right, you always did get me in trouble, Beck."

"Ignore her. Why did you ask about the mutilation, Mark?"

"It's nothing."

"Bullshit. We've got nothing. Talk to me."

"I really don't have any great insights, it's just as I read about the girls, I was reminded of what I witnessed in Africa. The village consisted of devout Muslims and they performed circumcision on girls." Mark took a long drink of water.

"What?" Beck asked.

"Come on, you've heard of the practice. Girls' genitals are cut, or mutilated. I'd see some of them after it was done. Their eyes were blank, like zombies. Only women did the cutting. I witnessed the worst of the practice because they were so poor. They used dirty razors, shards of glass, whatever was available and forget any pain killer or antiseptics. They'd use the same blood encrusted, disease ridden instrument over and over."

"They still do this?" Beck asked horrified.

"Of course. The reason for it is male domination. Has that ended? The point is to keep girls virginal until marriage and after marriage sex is so painful it forces women to remain faithful. It may be the new millennium, but for women in many parts of the world, it's the Dark Ages. Females remain bargaining chips for males. The insidious part of all of this is how women go obligingly to the knife to please their fathers, husbands, or some patriarch."

Beck looked at Mark as if he were a revelation. "Mark, you said this is practiced by devout Muslims?"

"Yeah, where I was but that's not the only religion that circumcises women," he answered.

"Do women have a choice in this?"

"Women? Hell, most of them are young girls, preteens," Mark's voice was touched with anger.

"What about young women, do they agree to this willingly?" Beck pushed.

"Choice is a tricky word when someone has been raised to think a certain way. They're brainwashed to accept it. This is just what I observed Beck, I'm not an authority, but a girl could not refuse. The cost was too heavy. Paying honor to the patriarch was a serious duty in that village. Refusal could get the girl beaten, maybe killed. The girls were afraid of being shunned. Shunning left a girl without the protection of her father, she might as well be dead. The reward is the emblem of purity. Even in this country we toy with the ideas of a woman's purity. Women still get married in white and wear veils. The words who gives this woman to this man is a relic of a father giving his chattel to another man. And that chattel had better have been a virgin. Lifting the veil was a symbol that sex could now occur without impunity and shame."

Beck drank her champagne slowly. "Yeah, you're right. Fathers and weddings. I'm glad I've had neither. Mark, I have to go. I have this thought developing in my head, and I have to let it make itself clear to me." Beck took her last gulp of champagne. "Please tell our easily offended friends that I apologize but I have to ditch the gossip and the cheesecake. Skipping the cheesecake will get their attention. You are brilliant. I will call you, I promise and thank you." Beck left the elegant room just as their dinners were being served.

****

While Beck almost dined in elegance; Will sweated in the drab, utilitarian precinct where once again the air conditioning was down. He blotted a drop of sweat off a file and watched as his perspiration blurred the M on the word murder. His sacred bodily fluid killed the word murder. He mused on bodily fluids, a phrase that took him to the joy of watching *Dr. Strangelove*. The memory gave him a portal out of the case and the office. Then the phone rang, obliterating any respite from reality. Reluctantly, Will answered, "Blake. Tommy? Been a while, yeah, what?" He paused. "Tommy boy, I swear, you better not be lying to me. Which park? Tillson, okay. I'll get back to you."

Will dialed the phone. "You get any report about a missing girl in Tillson Park? African American. No, I'll wait."

****

The endless drizzle created some impressive puddles in the potholes that crisscrossed the streets. Only a few intrepid pedestrians were out this late in that rain. The black SUV almost bottomed out in a pothole that looked more like a small valley. It kicked up rocks as it plowed through the water, its perfect polish was marred. It parked in the middle of the block, close to a bus stop. The driver's form was obscured by the pitch black windows and the darkness cast by the huge buildings that housed far too many people.

A bus stopped a half block away from the SUV. Ella appeared out of the cloud of exhaust created as the bus left its stop.

The driver got out of the SUV, holding and roughly petting a puppy. Ella adjusted her backpack, she looked around as Will had instructed. She waited by a lamppost for at least ten minutes. Finally, she started down the street, away from the SUV. A sharp yelp followed by a mournful howl echoed in the direction of the SUV. Ella ran toward the sounds of distress. She approached the SUV. She saw the puppy on the sidewalk, lifeless, its back legs lay in an opposite directions than its front legs. Ella gasped when she saw the twisted body. She gasped again when a shadow cast over her. Sadly, that was all she could do before she was picked up and thrown into the back of the SUV.

Thirteen

Beck's stereo and TV were on in her bedroom even though she worked on her desktop. The desktop was used for the serious work, when she was cocooned from the rest of the world. Her laptop was used for impulse shopping, looking up useless trivia. The two computers shared files. The TV showed Kate doing her job as a reporter. Kate stood by a barricade that kept protestors, mostly African Americans, contained in a small area. Many had signs bearing the message that Black children needed police protection and action. She turned to glance at the set to see the words Tillson Park and missing whiz by. She turned on the sound to Kate's voice. "The girl taken from Tillson Park has been identified as Erica Hubbard. She is fifteen years old, African American and lives in the projects next to the park. We have also learned that the body of a young woman, Ella King, also African American, seventeen, was found murdered early this morning."

Beck turned off the TV.

"Oh Jesus, Ella, why Ella, they, he, that son of a bitch must have followed us to Ella." Beck was unraveling, she knew it. She had to control herself. Every thought kept going to Safra. She typed in Richard Safra, Safra Inc., Wilder Agency. She typed in a code that Ann gave her on the sly.

The screen showed Sarfra/Wilder; then it went black.

"Oh no you don't, you son of a bitch, don't you dare crash on me." Right as Beck was going to punch the computer, the screen lit up with text. *Tic tock goes the clock. You have been caught breaching security and wasting time. You cannot find a person in a file. Do not fail, you don't want this to end like the LeMond case.*

Beck read the words but they did not seem like English. She couldn't comprehend that Safra had reached through her computer to terrorize her. She tried to delete but the words remained. Beck was spiraling into a very dark place. Each second she read the words were seconds closer to her losing control. She gawked at the computer like it was a gun that had misfired. She ripped the cord from the wall, ran into the living room and swooped up her laptop. Beck fled her apartment that had been wired and invaded by her own client. He got her back for that day she crossed the line by questioning him too closely.

***

Will ignored that there was a message from Beck on his phone. He was busy watching joggers in a park, the same park where Camille Davis' body was left drained of blood in a sandbox.

A man dressed in jeans, a T-shirt, motorcycle boots, covered in tattoos, sporting the obligatory shaved head, awkwardly jogged way toward Will.

"Tommy, I'm impressed. You're running and no one is chasing you." He quipped.

Tommy furled his middle finger at Will, then lit up a cigarette. "You're a real funny shit Blake. Ya wanna hear what I have to say or ya wanna keep doing bits for open mic night?" Will smiled. He walked toward a more secluded spot. "I'm listening."

"When are you guys goin' start humpin' this case of all them cut up little girls, Willie Boy? Lots of pissed off niggers, oh, I probably offended you."

Will rarely used Tommy as a Confidential Informant, he couldn't stand being around him but he was a damn good CI, reliable, and Will was desperate. "What do you know about it, Tommy?" he asked curtly.

"Stuff, good stuff, and it's goin' cost you, Blake. See, uh, I'm looking at some substantial time." He took a long hit of nicotine off his cigarette. The smart ass affect drained away.

"Be specific, Tommy you're wasting my humping time."

Tommy sniggered. He liked Will in spite of hating his being a homicide cop. Will was fair, he did what he said. "I need to shorten a dime's worth of time. There's a bullshit charge of me supposedly assaulting an officer during a drug bust. This is time I cannot do, Blake, can NOT do. So lucky me, I stumbled into some shit that I know you jokers could use concerning all these dead bodies pilin'up," Tommy jeered.

"Okay, what've you got?"

"Oh, no, no, no. You first." Tommy knew he had the cards.

Will quelled his frustration. "Did this assault that didn't happen include a weapon?" Will asked.

"A tiny, wussie assed dull knife, nothing," whined Tommy.

Will walked in a circle, he wanted to slug Tommy. "Jesus Tommy, another weapon's charge. I don't know. I don't know if I can move that."

Tommy pulverized the cigarette into the ground. "Fine, you live with the fact that maybe you could've caught the bastard who butchered all of them little girls but wouldn't try because of a kitchen knife."

"If what you tell me helps even the slightest, I will do everything I can. I'll go to bat for you."

Tommy looked at the young detective. He always wondered why someone who looked like a rock star was chasing jerks like him.

"You gonna swing that bat hard?"

"Babe Ruth," said Will.

"Ruth on steroids, Blake." They shook hands. Tommy always made Will shake his hand. There was some honor in Tommy's hard thirty-nine years of skin head gang life. "So, I have this acquaintance, no names. He conducts a certain kind of transaction out of his car. Parks are where he has lots of business. Tillson Park is one stop shopping for rich assholes who have a taste for white powders and various pills. They pretend to jog, hey like us, and like us they're out of place because that park ain't for yuppies or whatever you call rich young fucks these days. He noticed the black sedan. It went by him, lots. He thought maybe undercover cuz it wasn't the usual make of car of his clientele. They like German cars. He noticed it slowed down when it drove by the girl. He sees her get off the bench to go stand on the sidewalk. The car drives past her by just a few feet, stops. Then after a minute, the passenger door opened up and the kid jumped in. The girl went bye bye from Tillson and planet earth if you ask me."

They had walked quite a ways, Will wrote down every word Tommy said.

"Why didn't he call the cops?" Tommy couldn't help but slug Will in the arm.

"Did someone hit you in the head, officer? Or you just fucking stupid? Let me think, why was my friend in the park? Oh yeah, super cop, he was dealing. Yeah, he's going to call the cops about some kid getting in a car and stick around as a witness. And witness to what? Why the hell would anyone call the cops? The kid ran toward the car. No one dragged her in it. Coulda' been her parents for all anyone knew."

"Did he see the license plate?" Will asked sheepishly. Shit, Tommy was right, about everything.

"Naw, but he did see a ripped bumper sticker from a rental company. I wrote what he had down." Tommy gave Will the paper.

"It's not a whole name, but I can work with it. I gotta ask you Tommy, this guy, is he one of your Aryan brothers? You know all of these girls are black, and the working theory is this is racially motivated. Maybe this guy or maybe you want to put me on a wild goose chase away from the real suspects."

"Me?" Tommy was genuinely baffled.

"You did time for rape, you cut that white girl and you assaulted a black girl."

Tommy lit another cigarette, stopped walking, turned to Will. "First, I came to you, remember? Stupid move to out myself. Next, about the so-called rape. The lying bitch was white and she lied about her age. So yeah, I roughed her up, and maybe I cut her.

"You cut her vagina, Tommy," Will interrupted angrily.

"Come on Blake, it was her thigh. About the nigger. She ripped me off on a drug deal and she had a gun. I had a knife. I got no use for niggers but this shit that's going on is nowhere in my repertory. You need to catch the bastard, cut off his balls and put them in a blender for his last meal. You read me, Blake? Cuz me and some kids are countin' on ya."

Tommy never flinched, looked directly at Will as he spoke. Will believed him. He watched Tommy make his way through all the happy families and rich fucks as he called them. He knew Tommy was raised in violence and been treated like a dog his whole life. While Will contemplated the shitty hand millions of people are dealt, the sky opened up and poured tears, at least that's how Will thought of it.

***

When Will got to his car, he was drenched. Immediately the windows steamed up.

He rolled down the driver's side window and was hit by a torrent of rain. He tried to decide which was worse, the steamed up car or being soaking wet. He chose the steamed up car, turned on the defroster to full blast. He saw three missed calls from Beck; that worried him. Something had to be incredibly wrong. To get Beck to call once took Herculean effort; for her to leave a message, well, she didn't do that. He dialed. Beck's cell did not have a personal message, just some woman who must have made a fortune announcing the number that was dialed. "Beck, it's me. Call me as soon as you can. Are you okay?"

Then Will dialed another number. "Yeah, Blake here, I need some help with an informant. Great, yeah, I can be there in fifteen minutes."

***

Beck looked at the phone's lit screen, it read missed call WB. The coffee house was crowded with people waiting out the deluge of summer rain and wild lightning. The fresh baked bread and cookies, along with other amazing pastries were about to be put out for the second time. The first time was at the crack of dawn. The second shift of mouth-watering delicacies arrived whenever they got to it in the afternoon. It was kind of a contest to time being there right as things were coming out of the oven. So far round two had not arrived, but Beck wasn't there to gain weight. She was there because she knew this place was always crowded. For once Beck needed to be around people. She was there because it wasn't her apartment. She knew, or thought she knew, that it was a place that Safra could not get to her. Although she wasn't positive and that made Beck feel two things: first, it enraged her; second it scared her to her bones.

Beck took out her laptop. She hadn't opened it since the warning and accusation that she was responsible for the murdered girls appeared on the desktop. Shit, she wasn't an investigator. When she was a prosecutor the cops found the clues and the perps. She told Harvey she didn't want this job. Beck hoped the message was there. She wanted to show it to Will and Harvey. They needed to see that her own client was threatening her. He tampered with her computer, but how? That's what that intruder was doing in her place. Would they believe her? Why would he be pushing her like this? Did he want her to go over the edge? He knew she had a breakdown after LeMond; he offered revenge as a payment. Revenge against LeMond. How would he exact that revenge for her? She realized she savored the thought of that payment. No. No. No. She had to keep it straight; this was not about her.

Beck finally listened to the missed call from Will. Shit, he knew she's upset. No, she shouldn't show him Safra's message, not him or Harvey. Maybe they would say it was too much for her. Harvey could take her off the case, but Safra wouldn't let that happen. God, she needed him to keep her on the case but he was the one making her act—how was she acting? Her thoughts raced. She had to stop, she was making too much of all of this. It was simply a matter of being reprimanded for trying to break into an encrypted file. Nothing more, she couldn't let it be.

The pastries had arrived; a slight frenzy accompanied the aroma of melted butter baked into layers of flaky pastry and sugar. Beck snapped open her laptop. The screen came on. No message. She clicked on files, emails, nothing, nothing. For a moment she questioned whether the message ever existed. Enough. She had work to do; she'd call Will later, after she got the information she needed. Beck waved over a waitress. "May I have a large latte, two croissants, and three, no make that six chocolate nut cookies. Oh, and don't tally up the check, I probably will want a piece of cheesecake." Beck didn't care that the waitress whistled at the order. She was too busy typing the words female circumcision/genital mutilation in the search bar.

***

Beck ran up to the door right as the gray-haired woman was trying to lock it. Reluctantly Beck was allowed to enter the Women's Alliance Center even though it was well after closing.

"Thank you for letting me in, I know I am late. I intended to drive my car, but I can't find it." The woman looked confused. "I rarely drive. I use you know, the bus, or walk. So when I park it, I forget where because I use it so rarely. Um, look, are you Rachel?"

Another gray-haired woman approached them. "Are you Beck?"

"Oh, you must be Rachel, yes, I'm Beck Oldman. Thank you so much for seeing me this evening. I know I am keeping you."

"No, not at all. Evelyn, why don't you go home? I can lock up." Evelyn hesitated but after a reassuring nod from Rachel, she left them alone. Rachel escorted Beck through the office. They walked past posters of women from many cultures. Each poster had some message about women's rights or birth control. Scattered on every possible space were flyers touting shelters, child care, health centers and legal aid. They went by a room set up for children. Finally they sat down in a very small office that was crammed to the rafters with papers. The only tech to be seen was an outdated desktop computer. Beck seated herself on a very wobbly chair.

"We have very little funding, as you can see," apologized Rachel.

"Well, this country had to choose between women, children, and corporations. Billionaires are our priority, Rachel," Beck replied in mock seriousness.

"May I offer a compatriot coffee?" asked Rachel.

Beck was vibrating after her third latte and eating two pieces of cheesecake in addition to all of the pastries. Between the sugar and the caffeine she was ready to take flight.

"Uhh, no thank you, I think it may keep me from getting some sleep tonight."

"So, Beck, what can I help you with?" asked Rachel.

Beck hung onto her bag. She had ill-gotten gains, pictures that Will shouldn't have given to her. Forensic photos of Jasmine, Camille and Tamara.

"I need to know about the practice of genital mutilation," Beck asked anxiously.

Rachel tried to size up the small, very intense woman. It was the strain in Beck's voice that enticed Rachel to let her come so late. She was convinced she was talking to a junkie or a mental patient. Beck would be impressed at Rachel's assessment. She valued good instincts even if those instincts were insulting.

"Why so urgent?" Rachel asked, gently.

Beck was aware that caffeine heightened her high octane intensity. She fought to be calm, but that only made her seem more off.

"I don't know if you watch TV. Let me start at the beginning." She took a breath. "I have been working with the homicide division, well one detective. I'm a private detective; I used to be a prosecutor." Again she stopped, breathed. "Look, Rachel if you could just tell me what I asked then I could explain why I am here, because maybe I shouldn't be here. I may be on the wrong track, see?"

No, Rachel did not see at all, but she decided that Beck's plan, oddly, was a good one.

"Well, Beck, the bottom line of why it's done is to control women. Women's sexuality has historically been problematic for men in just about all cultures. There were chastity belts. Women were locked up during their menstrual cycle because they were thought to be unclean; it was a time of shame. People who take the Bible literally believe that women were assigned a special penalty for Eve eating the apple, bearing children in pain and suffering a monthly curse. Women in literature are portrayed as the temptress. So, different times, different cultures do what they do to control women. Freud advocated controlling women in his book *Sexuality and the Psychology of Love* through female circumcision. He believed it was necessary for the development of femininity. Interestingly he thought having his sons undergo circumcision was too painful and unnecessary for their masculinity."

"I knew Freud had issues with women, but circumcision?" Beck asked surprised.

"He postulated that women felt cheated by not having a penis and that the clitoris needed to be eliminated allowing women a mature orgasm. Clitoral orgasm, according to a man who did not possess a clitoris, was an immature response."

"So Freud's prescription is to cut it off and grow up unless what is being cut is a penis. I remember in a lit class discussing that often the underlying message in stories written by men was that women were the sexual aggressor, that men weren't the ones with the constant hard-on's. Sorry, Rachel."

Rachel waved off her apology. "Have you checked out what is happening across the country? The attack on women's contraception. Like I said, new times, new methods, same old story. You wanted to know about genital mutilation associated with Muslim practice?"

Beck nodded.

"Well, in very traditional communities it is the norm. It is seen as paying homage to the father or patriarch. There is so much to explain about this practice. It is mixed with religion and superstition in less sophisticated parts of the world. For example some believe the clitoris is dangerous to the male partner."

"That's not a superstition, that's a fact," retorted Beck. The women shared a moment of quiet solidarity.

"I feel like I am shooting in the dark to get you what you want, Beck. It's time you tell me why you are here."

Beck spread the photos on the desk.

"I shouldn't have these. I hope you will not let anyone know you've seen them because it will get a very good guy in trouble."

Rachel put on her glasses to study the pictures. She left the room without a word.

Beck didn't know what to think, so she thought the worst. Shit, she's calling the cops, or maybe she knows who I am, crap, she's calling Harvey. Does this place have the money for a security guard? Before Beck could create another pessimistic scenario, Rachel returned with pictures of her own, she laid them next to Beck's. There was very little difference between them. Beck's eyes were question marks.

"These girls in these photographs underwent what is called infibulation. It is the most severe form of circumcision. Look at your pictures, more than a rough approximation, wouldn't you say?" asked Rachel. "In my photos the girls underwent this procedure with crude instruments. The cutting in your pictures shows someone with a modicum of skill. Certainly not a doctor."

Beck was shocked. "A doctor? What doctor would do this?"

"Many, not in this country, or at least not publicly advertising it. Wealthy people have the means to hire a doctor who is of like mind. The girl will have a better chance to avoid the complications and may have the luxury of anesthesia."

"Do you know of any doctors I can speak to? Anyone I can talk to about doing this practice here?"

"No, this is done in secret. It's underground behavior."

"What about women in their teens or older? I was told it still is done on them."

"Yes. Maybe you can find an adult woman to speak with. I know of no one. They of course make the choice and so it is an easier road, legally and morally for those who perform circumcision. It eliminates accusations of child abuse. Still, I believe women are coerced into the practice." Rachel looked at her watch, Beck got the signal. "May I borrow these photographs?" asked Beck.

"First, tell me what you haven't Beck."

"The pictures I brought are of murdered girls who have been in the news. I was hired to find one of the girls, I failed. Now I am trying to find the maniac who did this and I'm also looking for Olivia Safra."

"Is Olivia Safra a Muslim? Is that what brought you here?" asked Rachel.

"I have a gut reaction that there is a connection. My gut is rarely wrong. May I borrow these photographs?"

"Yes, Beck, and if there is anything I can do to help you, call me," said Rachel. She meant the offer. Rachel could see that Beck cared for the murdered girls at her own peril.

****

Will kept hitting Beck's door. Rapid fire knocks replaced single shots, replaced by banging incessantly. He dialed her number again. The annoying robotic voice informed him for the millionth time what number he had dialed. He was irritated. Will was never irritated. He could be furious, passionate, sardonic, but not irritated; this was a new feeling that appeared when he started to spend time with Beck. Finally, he left, extremely irritated.

***

Beck couldn't have known that she had just missed Will when she entered her home. She did her usual scan of the apartment, checking to see if anything was out of its place, which was quite a feat in that chaos. Beck did the usual getting acclimated to being home, including grabbing old food that was not put away. She found half of a sandwich on the counter. Things had been more orderly for a while, Will's presence had done that to her, but lately the apartment was the reflection of her true state of being. She flopped down on the sofa. Her head was spinning from all that happened and what she gleaned from Rachel. Pieces of a weird puzzle were snapping together. She had to take notes, organize her thoughts. Beck knew that when she spoke to Will and Harvey she needed to be very clear, linear. What she wanted to present was nothing more than her gut feeling and it couldn't sound the way she feared, insane. No matter how hard she tried to dispel the crazy, it clung relentlessly. She comforted herself with her belief that crazy doesn't mean wrong.

Beck started to organize the photographs but something stopped her. Something gnawed at her. She wanted to call Will, but she didn't and she couldn't figure out why. She had to use the desktop, this was serious work. Beck gathered up her things and moved into the bedroom.

Finally she was ready to turn the computer on and get to it. She hit the button, the screen started up ready for action. Then her eye caught something glinting off the keyboard. She knew what it was instantly, intuited it, faster than her eyes could transmit the image to the brain and the brain form the word. Beck reached out as if she were in danger of being bitten. She picked it up. Yes, it was the one. The same color smeared on the bullet. Isn't that what they called lipstick tubes, bullets? This was the lipstick she tossed in the garbage, miles away, at night. When? A week, more?

Weirdly, Beck didn't feel afraid; fury killed fear. She felt the kind of fury that makes people buy weapons and use them to invoke the kind of terror that no one wants to imagine. After all, isn't that what was being done to her? Then, that exact terror began to seep in through the monitor.

A woman in a room appeared. At first glance the woman looked like Beck, just older. Beck recognized her. A nurse entered the room. She struggled to make the woman take pills, after a hard won success, she left. The room had several beds. The disheveled woman spit out the medicine, stuck it under the mattress of another bed. When she turned, she faced the camera. Paused, like she was getting her picture taken.

Beck froze until Safra's voice shattered her trance. *Your poor aunt, Rebekkah. How old was she when she was afflicted by mental illness? I am very worried about you. You are stealing like you did during the LeMond case, does this mean you are about to commit some irreversible error again? You've been wasting so much time speaking to that woman and Mr. Ibish. Rebekkah, did I make a mistake entrusting you with my case?*

Beck wanted to curl up into the fetal position; she wanted to smash the computer into a thousand pieces; she wanted to kill Richard Safra. She wasn't sure which one she would find herself doing when she left the apartment.

***

The pounding of Beck's heart matched each foot that pounded the ground. She ran down block after block. The rain was letting up but she was soaked. Where the hell did she put her car? When did she use it last? Christ. It was late, she realized if a police car came by they would stop her. She gathered up the last of her control and walked casually. The thought struck her, yes, by the flower shop. It was such a great spot so close to her place, but now she had to loop back. She felt relieved when she spotted the car. See, she thought, I am okay. I'm not my aunt.

***

Beck sat in her car in front of the all-night grocery store. She threw her backpack to the floor then lowered her head onto the steering wheel. The sounds that came from her were not exactly cries but they were sounds of distress.

***

Now it was Will's door being assaulted by incessant knocking. Beck could see she had awakened him. She had lost all sense of time. "Where have you been? I've been trying to get you all day," he said. She barged past him. She had never been there before. Will's apartment was very neat with lots of plants and original art on the walls. Piles of books, too many for the shelves, even more CD'S and vinyl records.

Will ran his hand through his hair in an effort to wake up. Beck paced. She nodded her head frenetically. Will decided to let Beck tell him what was wrong, rather than inquire.

Beck pointed to some art hanging on the wall. "You painted those?"

"Yeah, a long time ago." He said still groggy.

"You're good, really good, and look at all of these plants. They're so healthy. I tried plants, they died."

Will sat down; he figured maybe if he sat she would slow down. Beck tossed her backpack next to him. She kneeled down to go through his records. "God, I love Pink Floyd, did we already discuss that?"

"Beck?"

"What time is it?" she asked.

"Two."

She was bewildered. The last she remembered it was early evening.

"Beck, what's happened?" Will's voice was thin with fear.

"He's everywhere, Will. Everywhere. He may be here too Will, check your computer and your phone."

"Who, Beck? Who's everywhere? Beck, look at me, talk to me."

Beck handed Will the lipstick. "A dead woman wouldn't wear that shade. Maybe that's why he gave it back to me, a hint of what's in the cards. I threw it away, far away from my computer, miles in fact, but there it was. It was there and so was my dear Aunt Becky. My namesake, my titular hero. The sweetest most screwed over human on planet earth. She's been in a mental institution forever but not tonight."

Will leaned forward like people do when they show they're really listening or because they think the leaning will help them to understand. "I'm not getting what you mean. I must not be fully awake yet."

"He had me followed. It was a damn good thing I lost my car, but I found it so I could drive here. He followed me, that's how he got the lipstick." She said in a conspiratorial tone.

Beck tugged on her hair, she knew she wasn't being clear, being linear and this wasn't even the hard thing to convey.

"I feel naked. He is skinning me alive with my own life. Ella, Will, he got Ella. He got Olivia. He owns all the technology, spyware, even what the cops use. He made it clear he could get to me, he wired my computer, my apartment and…"

"Lipstick, your aunt, Ella? Spies? I need help here," begged Will.

Beck dumped her backpack out on the floor. A package of batteries, a candy bar, and a bottle of maple syrup lay in front of her. Will was incredulous.

"Shoplifting? You'll be crucified if you're caught, we both will. I'm a cop." Will said sharply.

Beck cocked her head, this remark quieted her. "Then arrest me, or maybe you want to have me committed."

"Knock it off Beck, now," he demanded.

His demand, that touch of anger was needed; it helped her, so carefully, without emotion she said, "Safra is getting to me, getting all of us."

"Getting us?"

"I think Ella was killed by Safra, or let me be clear, his thugs, because he is the man behind the curtain controlling events. He's responsible for Olivia's death. Ella is closer to Olivia's age so when they find Olivia she will fit the pattern. Do you know what female circumcision is, Will? Girls who have that done to their bodies look exactly like the dead girls. They're mutilated the same way."

Beck rummaged through the backpack, got the pictures Rachel gave her and the forensic photos. She spread them out and pointed for Will to look at them.

"See? These are pictures of girls from Africa who had this horrible thing done to them. They are Muslim and that is one of the major religions that believe in this practice and Safra is a practicing Muslim except he defiles the religion because he's a murdering thug."

Slowly Will feared and loathed her outlandish theory. It struck him that Beck had said those were the feelings she inspired in cops. "What do you mean he's following you?" He asked skeptically.

She held the lipstick up. "I stole this. I threw it away in a bus stop trash bin, but it was on my keyboard tonight. I tried to get into his files. The next thing I knew my monitor had a message on it, warning me to get back to Olivia's case." Beck struggled but maintained her composure. "I have an aunt who is ill, I told you that Will," she needed to calm down. "There was a video feed or whatever it's called from her hospital. I saw her for the first time in years but it was Becky. A narration accompanied the movie. Safra, telling me that I was going to end up like my aunt. He knew where I was today. He knew that I spoke to Rachel, the woman who gave me the pictures. He warned me Will. This is all a warning. He didn't like that I found out about this butchering that goes on in the name of his religion."

"And you think what?"

"Are you trying to be stupid, Will?"

"No, I'm not trying to be stupid. I'm trying not to put words in your mouth. I want you to tell me what you think, exactly." He answered calmly.

Beck stood up. "I think, Detective Blake, that bastard had his daughter undergo that slaughter and she died. Harvey thinks she's dead. We all do. She's been gone too long. Think what a publicity nightmare it would be for that prick if people knew he was responsible for his daughter to be butchered like that. And, I think, he, that, he, uh—he had those girls murdered to cover up what happened to Olivia."

Will fell back on the floor, put his hands over his eyes. His head hurt.

"Jesus, Beck, how did you get to this?"

"I'm seeing with the eyes of the killer, Will, isn't that what I'm supposed to do?" She regretted her tone and sarcasm. "Will. Olivia will be found and she will just be another in the body count of murdered and mutilated females," she intoned flatly.

"If Olivia died because of this monstrous procedure, and he wanted to hide it, he could have just gotten rid of her body. You know that's right," insisted Will.

"No. He had to report her missing or that would have been suspicious, and because of who he is, the case was high profile. His back was against the wall. He had to look like he gives a damn, so he hired Harvey. He would be dogged forever if she went Amelia Earhart and he had done nothing. Olivia's body has to be found, a victim of the serial killer. Then he can be the grieving father we know that he's not. It's perfect. He will be free of the cops and the Press. Safra can milk a lot of goodwill from the murder of his daughter. It has to be him, Will. Not one clue? Only a many headed monster like Safra can pull this off."

Will gently massaged Beck's shoulders as he spoke. "Actually, I think I caught a break. You know we got some calls about black sedans cruising the parks and the basketball courts, but no one could identify the model. Today I got a lead. Someone saw the Hubbard girl get into a car at Tillson. A torn bumper sticker from a rental company was seen. This guy is smart, rent a car, never two of the same model, something modest. We're alerting rental agencies around the city," said Will.

Beck shook her head, "Well that doesn't mean…"

"What Safra is doing to you has to be stopped. Quit. He's a ghoul, a dangerous one, agreed, but come on Beck, slaughtering randomly chosen girls from the projects to hide at worst an unethical medical procedure? Maybe he did kill Olivia, but that's separate from Jasmine and the others. Last point, I haven't gotten a report that Ella was mutilated."

Beck heard the million voices in her head simultaneously; it made her think of Poe's *The Tell-Tale Heart* where the narrator heard everything in heaven and in hell. Crazy. Crazy theory.

Will led Beck to the sofa. There was a large throw begging for them to bundle themselves in its warmth. Will obliged.

"My anger and fear of Safra has taken me down the rabbit hole to a revenge theory," she said in a defeated voice.

Will swung her legs over his lap. "Beck, he's a killer, we know that, but he didn't kill the girls. He didn't have his thugs kill the girls; they're not connected." He caught a glimpse of the ill-gotten gains on the floor. "How about you stay here tonight, let me take care of you? I could use some knight in shining armor practice, if you'll let me."

Beck melted into his arms. She was hungry for his mouth, maybe through a kiss she could become whole, or at least cut the million voices by half.

Fourteen

Harvey was a pro at conveying fury. He could have been the template for old Warner Brothers cartoon characters. The ones with steam coming out of their ears, or their hair blowing off the top of their heads; pitch forks in their eyes. This scary huffing and puffing was one of the many things that made him such a successful homicide detective. People believed he would deliver on the spoken, or worse, the unspoken threats. This persona never worked on Beck. She was as volatile as he was, and to be truthful, while he knew he wouldn't deliver anything that matched his bravado, he was not so sure about Beck. Her gutsy unpredictability was one of the things that made him adore her while simultaneously wanting to pummel her to the ground. Beck was a porcupine, always shooting off quills to keep people away from her soft underbelly. Most people didn't spend the time or see anything in her that was worth taking her crap or living up to her impossible standards. So in spite of his age and all the weird bullshit surrounding Blake, Harvey respected him for his tenacity and vision to care about the tormented and brilliant person sitting before him. Harvey hated that he was going to add more to Beck's overflowing cup of pain, so to cover his own, he affected the cartoon Harvey.

Beck was mentally exhausted, but what she liked to call her auxiliary brain kept her going. Two nights ago she came as close to melting down as she ever had, far worse than during LeMond. That only triggered shoplifting. Safra's dogging her and her belief that he was involved in the murders, in spite of Will's rational rebuttal, pushed Beck close to a break. The kind of break that found one in a hospital gown like her aunt's. She was getting impatient with the seemingly pissed off Harvey. He was way below his usual game of intimidation. Probably because Safra, she surmised, had publicly and privately castrated him. Wow, there's that idea again, genital mutilation by Safra, delivered by the knife or his owning you. Bastard.

"Safra knows you tried to get into his files again," started Harvey.

"Yeah, because he spies on me, he's all over me, Harvey. He's got it backwards; I'm supposed to be looking under every rock to find his daughter. He's not supposed to be having me followed, taping my phones, worse, wiring my home, my computer. I want out of this nightmare you dreamed up for me."

"How many times are we going to sing that song? No one knew you worked for me when he pulled that announcement at the conference. I never wanted you on this case, Beck, so stop the bullshit."

"You're an owner in this agency, Harvey. You let him take over your company and let him blindside me. We're supposed to have each other's backs against…"

The landline phone rang. Harvey's face said it all, Beck was about to be blindsided again and this time, Harvey knew it. He answered the phone. "Hello. Yes, she is."

Harvey switched on the speaker. His voice took her back to the shock of seeing her aunt on her computer. She felt violated again.

"Harvey, give Beck the envelope," Safra commanded.

Harvey took a large envelope from a drawer, handed it to Beck whose eyes conveyed hurt and betrayal. Harvey had to look away.

"Open it, Rebekkah. Read your bank and credit card statements," demanded Safra.

Beck dropped the envelope on her lap, unopened.

"You will see, when you finally open the envelope, (he paused) that your shopping habits have put you into thousands of dollars in debt, make that tens of thousands. You tried to trade your compulsions. Stealing replaced by out of control shopping. It hasn't worked, has it? You're back at it Beck. Syrup? Arrested for stealing syrup would be even worse than hardware."

Beck glared at Harvey. "Are you going to say something, Harvey?" Harvey looked up at the ceiling.

"Rebekkah no one likes to have their personal files or life pried into but your business is mine until you find her. I own your time and you have been wasting it. You waste it by stealing lipsticks and going to women's centers. Harvey, if you can't control our employees…"

Harvey wasn't faking his anger, "You're stealing again? You're fired." Beck didn't have a chance to be confused, or betrayed, or angry, or quit before Safra's irritation bled through his unctuous voice.

"That will mean more time wasted. She knows the case. Rebekkah, I will pay off your debts, make you wealthy, and will pay you as I offered. Revenge is very sweet. Find her. Do it discreetly. My life is not to be part of your investigation. Do this, or I fear for your mental health. Harvey, I will call you later." Click. Gone was the voice of Lucifer.

Beck threw the envelope at Harvey. "I quit you son of a bitch." She tried to get to the door before he grabbed her by the arm.

"You think you can quit? Try it and Kate will be announcing the mysterious disappearance of the infamous former district attorney, or maybe you'll end up in a coma, or maybe there will be a ceremony where Safra scatters the ashes of the intrepid investigator who was murdered trying to find his daughter. That would get him lots of great publicity. You choose, Beck. There's only one way out of this. You find that kid or the son of a bitch who murdered her, so we, you and me, can end this with they lived, forget the happily ever after."

Beck struggled to get loose of his grip. "Why did he say our employees?"

"Because one of my asshole partners has a gambling debt. Of course Safra has connection to Atlantic City. He generously offered this very partner a free trip to stay at one of his casinos. He ran up the inevitable debt which was settled by the partner's share of this agency transferred to Safra."

He dragged Beck to her chair, pushed her down. "Now you tell me what the hell is going on, so we have a chance to survive this nightmare."

***

Will was on the phone when three cops dragged Tommy Justin past his desk. Tommy tried to get free to attack Will but they yanked him away by his handcuffs. Will threw the receiver down, stormed over to Tommy.

"What the hell is he doing here?" he demanded.

"Like you fucking don't know, Blake," snarled Tommy.

"I don't, I don't know, Jim here is about to tell me."

Jim laughed, leaned back in his chair. His weight ballooned his gut far over his belt. The years of working with death, corruption, and perverts took a toll on his health. Jim looked like he had maybe a few years before the unavoidable heart attack or stroke.

"Your snitch fits, like a glove, to the profile of the killer. His weapon of choice is a knife, he cuts people, Will. Ol' Tommy has been arrested for rape, he's a known racist, and he knew Hubbard was gone before her aunt called missing persons. You've been blowing off the department's official motive, racism. You've done nothing to check out pedophiles but you did talk to Tommy, didn't you? Turns out you're not so stupid because you pretty much gave him to us."

Will contained himself; he knew that if he acted even on a fraction of what he was feeling, he would lose any chance of getting answers.

"How do you know I saw Tommy? Have I been followed by my fellow detectives?"

Tommy watched the irony of the whole scene. The cop that was supposed to help him was on the ropes. He knew Will as much as the criminal can know the cop, which wasn't much. But what he did know, like Einstein knew math, was a double cross, a set-up, a betrayal. Will was about to get all three of those lessons in one short minute. Will had nothing to do with his arrest, it was obvious and that terrified Tommy. He realized at that minute he had a snowball's chance in hell of getting out of there, like he wanted, alive.

Purified

"Well?" demanded Will. "Are you following me? Is my phone tapped?" The thought hit him that maybe he should not have dismissed Beck's fears so quickly.

"You've been thinking with your dick, not with your Ivy League waste of time education. How can you be with her? She's old, crazy, and a traitor."

Will towered over Jim. His youth, intellect, and compassion made Jim feel small.

"So because of your hatred of Oldman, this department makes an arrest that you know is wrong? Are the gears in motion to hold him as the sacrificial goat? For what? More importantly, for who? This isn't just dirty, this is letting a serial killer go free, a killer of children, and you fucking know it. You know it." All of the anger in Will was replaced by the horror of what good men were capable of doing.

Will turned to Tommy. "I'll do what I can to fix this. I swear it."

Tommy sunk into his chair. Poor Will, he thought, he was as screwed as he was. He relished the fifteen minutes before he was arrested because he knew they were his last minutes of freedom.

Fifteen

There were very few people milling about the student quad in front of the Student Union. The summer session was closing, the stifling weather drove people to inside amusements and the lucky were out of town. Beck looked like a student in her jeans, T-shirt, sneakers, and backpack. Her hair hadn't been cut in ages. It grew fast and the shaggy length made her look even younger. One would have to get very close to her to realize she wasn't a kid. Her eyes were old, aged from the inside out. She had waited for a long time, one foot up against the wall eased her fatigue. Finally, there he was.

"Mustafah," she called out. She worked on the tone, a request not a bark.

When he saw who called, Mustafah sped up his retreat from the campus. Of course Beck pursued him.

"Please stop and speak with me. I promise, it will be short and nothing like the last time."

He looked to see if anyone was around. He was afraid. "I've said too much."

"Someone spoke to you about seeing me," she guessed.

"No, no one spoke to me," he was very careful with his words.

Beck pointed to a grassy area where there were a lot of trees. "Go over there. I'll meet you." She was relieved that he acquiesced so easily. In a few minutes she joined him. They were obscured from the street and most of the quad.

"I think, Mustafah, you knew Olivia a lot better than you let on, and that's why someone has warned you, or said something that clearly has you concerned about talking to me."

Mustafah pawed the wet leaves.

"Did you know that she had been circumcised?"

Without looking up or interrupting his attack on the leaves Mustafah asked, "Which time?"

Beck grabbed his forearm. "What do you mean, which time?"

Once he again he searched to see if someone was watching them. "It was done when she was a child, I have no idea how old she was. That was the first time. She said she was going to have it done again before the marriage. She told us like it was a credential that proved her devoutness to her religion. It alienated her from the few other women who came to meetings."

"Marriage, what are you talking about?"

Now it was his turn to look at her with shock. "How did you not know that? I thought you were working to find her. That you worked for her fath--I thought you were an investigator. I have said too much, yet again."

Mustafah left the nook of trees to the openness of the quad. Beck followed him, then she saw Jamal. Beck managed to catch up with Mustafah while making it look casual. She smiled as she spoke to him. "Keep walking. You need to do what I say and don't argue or ask questions. Start to walk faster, just get a little ahead of me, like you're trying to get away from. His bones told him to obey her. She let him get just a few feet ahead. She looked frustrated that he was moving away, but she was close enough for him to hear her. "I'm going to give you a lesson on street theatre. On the count of ten, stop walking, look at me. You'll love this part, scream at me to get away from you, that you had nothing to say to me before, nothing now, and nothing ever. If I ever approach you again, you'll call campus security. You make it real, like your life depended on it, because it just might."

On the count of ten precisely, Mustafah stopped in his tracks, glared at Beck with genuine hatred.

"I told you never to contact me again. I have nothing to say to you ever, not in this life or the next one. You are an insult to everything I hold sacred. You are an infidel bitch and if you try to bother me, I'll call the campus cops," he bellowed.

Beck watched as he stomped out of sight. Well, if Jamal didn't believe he hated Beck, she did. She did a bit of acting too, appeared shocked, afraid. Beck's cell rang; this time she answered. "Will, wait, okay, you sound awful. Yes, I know the place, I can be there in say twenty minutes."

After stuffing the cell in her pocket, Beck wanted to wave to Jamal, but he was gone. She thought she deserved an Academy Award for best direction of a fake fight, or at least a nomination by her audience who was so convinced, he abandoned his post. Beck decided to walk rather than catch the bus. Her car was still parked at Will's. She hoped she would remember where it was, great parking spots were useless if you can't remember where you parked your car.

***

It was busy outside the campus. The low rumbling thunder heralded an end to the welcomed hours of summer sun. An audible groan arose from the walkers. Traffic was thick and slow, just like the air. As Beck moved with the crowd toward the crosswalk, she felt something behind her. Someone was too close. It was hell being a small person in these human crushes, there was always someone up her ass. They were about to move as a herd but she managed to work her way to the curb, first. Here the traffic didn't seem to move so slowly. The presence returned. She had enough of being handled. As she turned to tell the molester to back off, she faced Jamal. He smiled as he pushed her off the curb into the flow of cars and trucks. She fell flat on her back. An SUV barreled right toward her, slammed on the brakes just inches from Beck, then sped off. Luckily the light had changed. A man ran out to help her back to the sidewalk. Everyone remarked what a close call she just had and where was the bastard who had pushed her.

***

Beck inhaled the dank air; she loved the malty, oaky smell of the bars but she no longer missed the heavy hit of tobacco and smoke. It was pretty crowded for a workday but this place had three-star air conditioning. She spied Will in the corner. When she got to his table, he stood up and pulled her close to him. He held her very tightly. This was not affection; this was need. He crushed her. She had to push away to catch a breath. He hung his head to his chest. This was a Will she had never seen. Beck gently kissed him on each check and his mouth. It was if they had reversed roles from the other night. This scared her far more than anything Safra had done to her.

They sat at the small table. Will already ordered two beers, the bottles were sweating even with the air conditioning. She waited for him to talk.

"I was, or maybe still am, being followed by the cops I work with. When I first joined I had a partner but it became clear that I worked better on my own. I mean if there's a bust or something like that Jim and I go out, we're officially teamed but I'm mostly alone. I'm too weird for conventional cops, hell too weird for conventional anybody. It worked, for the most part. People let me be me. I'm productive, no, I'm damn good at my job. So even though they aren't in love with me, they accepted me with certain conditions. They know my sister was murdered and the guy got away with it. It's one of the reasons they cut me some slack. I became a cop for revenge, for doing good, or who the fuck knows why. I believe in the job and the people who do it with me."

Will gulped the entire beer in a single breath. Beck poured her beer in a glass. Another role reversal.

"They followed me to my snitch. The guy who gave me the tip about the rental car. He's a skinhead, a racist who has cut females. Some of his crew have been convicted for murder. He hasn't ever been brought in as a suspect for murder. Now he's sitting in county waiting to be served up as the serial killer. It's so fucking ludicrous. Who's going to believe it?"

Beck didn't answer, she wasn't sure she should but his look indicated he had not asked a rhetorical question. "Everyone," she answered.

"What?"

"You asked who's going to believe that your snitch is guilty. I said everyone."

Will shifted uncomfortably on the hard wood chair. "So overnight I go from a good cop to a bad one? That I let my CI walk from a murder wrap? Or that I am too stupid to figure out he's the perp? How, how do they make that stick?"

"You know how. They painted you with the Oldman brush. I told you, fear and loathing."

Will shook his head, "No, no there's more."

Beck didn't relish going back to their conversation. Will was convinced she was wrong, so convinced he made her see the error of her ways, but maybe if she could get him to see the power of Safra he could stop tearing himself to pieces.

"Remember Mustafah, the student I spoke to?" Will grunted in affirmation.

"He told me that Olivia Safra was engaged."

"Engaged? To whom? Safra knew about this guy and never told the cops, you, or Harvey? What the fuck?"

"Yeah, what the fuck. Who is the potential son-in-law and where the hell has he disappeared to? Why didn't he ever come forward? Bet you a million Safra bucks he's vanished into some country that doesn't extradite to the good ol' USA."

"No way to prove what this kid said is right if Safra denies it," Will said, dejectedly.

"Oh, he's going to deny it. You know why? Because Olivia had another circumcision done for Daddy and her future husband."

"Another?" asked Will.

"Yes, Mustafah said she told him it was done to her when she was a little girl. So that means in Africa. Well, that wasn't good enough or maybe the act of doing it to honor father and fiancé had to be completed, or maybe she didn't have the most drastic cutting, infibulation, done to her as a child."

Beck drank the rest of the beer before she continued.

"Here's how I figure it. Harvey was hired to make Safra appear to be the concerned parent. Then he does this weird thing. He insists on hiring the pariah of the police force and the city, me. Why? Because my shitty reputation is exactly what he needed. No one would believe he was linked to these murders if it was my theory. Then, score, you and I work together. Safra didn't see that coming. How lucky could he get that the one cop who didn't drop kick me out of the station was the guy who had his own issues, another loner, another rule breaker."

"Yes, Beck, our reputations are crap. How does that make him a killer?"

"Before I saw Mustafah today, I went to the university library, figured the bastard couldn't wire those computers. I looked up the public record on Safra's politics. Do you know how much money he pours into the most pro-abortion, contraception rights senator in existence? A fortune. Why? Because she grants his tech companies, all of his companies, contract after government contract. They are in political bed together. The one thing that could get his ass kicked out of those sheets is if she found out that he forced his daughter to undergo that barbaric, misogynistic mutilation."

Will could not hide his disdain. "He murdered Olivia, and covered her murder with the killing of the other girls for political gain?" Beck decided to overlook Will's sarcastic tone.

"Power and politics is all he cares about. He doesn't just dislike her, he loathes her. She's a constant reminder that he doesn't have a son. Male dominance is a big deal to him. The last thing he could tolerate is being destroyed by a female politician because of what he had done to his female offspring. For him, that would be worse than death by a thousand cuts. Hmm, probably not the best reference."

Beck's theory disturbed him.

"Beck, all he had to do was hide Olivia's body. You're not even saying that he killed Olivia. You're saying at worst, he forced her to have this procedure. How? She's over eighteen. All he has to say is that she chose to undergo circumcision and it went terribly wrong. Beck, if he's the great and evil Oz, he could handle Olivia without slaughtering kids that have nothing to do with him."

There he had her. She couldn't square it, she just knew it. She just intuited Safra's complicity in the murder of Jasmine and the others.

"I don't know, Will, I don't know how to explain that piece. Maybe he physically dragged her to some butcher and it went wrong and he didn't get help. Maybe there was a witness, someone who escaped his tentacles and is hiding. Maybe Olivia decided to rebel and go public about what her father made her do, maybe threaten to go to the Senator. You have to admit what you saw in those pictures of the murder victims and those who had circumcision are practically identical. It's more than a wild, weird coincidence. And, why is he after me? Every step I make that might lead to an answer about Olivia, he gaslight's me." Will looked perplexed.

"*Gaslight*, old movie, this guy tries to make a sane woman thinks she's going insane by screwing with the gas in the lights. God, we do have an age difference." Beck sank back in her chair.

"I can't answer why that maniac does what he does. I told you to quit. I've also told you about a million times, the girls' profiles do not match Olivia Safra's," argued Will.

"Ella was almost seventeen. I think we led him to her." The fear and anger in his eyes scared Beck. She didn't mean to say that to him. He was fragile and she was frustrated.

"Ella was not taken; she was murdered, dumped, and not cut. But if you're right, that I put the maniac onto her, then I am worse than the cops who did nothing about my sister," he whispered the word sister.

Beck tried to put her hand on Will's; he recoiled. His next words were sent like bullets.

"I think this has taken a toll on you, Beck. That's the only explanation for this theory. You blame yourself for Jasmine's death. It wasn't your fault but the weight of that and your past has taken a toll."

Beck retracted her hand. "Toll, what do you mean, toll? A toll that could make someone crazy? Like her aunt? Safra was ingenious and you are proving it. Any theory of mine linking him to his daughter's death would be dismissed because it came from me, because I suffered a toll. Wow. So did I come up with this because I'm an angry, unstable woman seeking revenge against anyone handy? Maybe. Still, it doesn't answer why Safra's thug followed me to the university today and shoved me into the oncoming traffic." Will was stunned. Why didn't you?"

"Tell you? Because I could see you were in more trouble than I was. Who knew that the first person to prove my theory about Safra would be you?"

Beck picked up a bottle; she contemplated throwing the contents on him, instead she walked away. Will drank the rest of her beer, waved the waitress over for another round.

***

Beck walked at a very brisk pace. This was the best part, the part that gave her the pure adrenalin high, it took over and she had no choice, no free will. Getting out of the store with the item and into her car was the climax. She had taken a cab from the bar to Will's neighborhood. This time she knew exactly where her car was parked. She started for home but the weird advertisement, a tall balloon like giant Gumby that flailed wildly, lured her into the strip mall. Big sales were on until ten PM. If she couldn't steal with some jeopardy of being caught then she was a failure. Feeling like a failure drove her to steal. It made her take reckless chances. She anticipated the day where she could overcome the impulse and choose to leave whatever she picked up because she was in control, because she wanted to. She got in the car and removed men's shoes from her feet, tossed them on the passenger seat. She left behind her favorite sneakers but that was the only way she could get out of there. Damn, she liked those sneakers. She hesitated to start the car. The high was beginning to dissipate and she would be left alone with guilt and self-recrimination.

Beck started the car and turned on the radio. She pulled straight out of the space. She always tried to park the car away from other cars. That way she didn't have to back out. She drove by the creepy Gumby, falling to its knees then shooting back up. What deranged person created those things? Those were thoughts Beck wanted to ponder, not Jasmine, Olivia, Safra, or

Will, not Will most of all. Beck turned onto the main street. She drove slowly; her thoughts were beginning to escalate. She decided to drive through the neighborhoods. She looked in the rear view mirror as she changed lanes to turn left. Slowly, a dark figure arose from the back seat. It all took place in slow motion. Somehow she didn't scream. All she could think was don't stop driving, no matter what. The figure held a knife and was moving toward Beck. A couple walking a dog yelled after the car to slow down. She drove erratically, veering the car sharply to the right and left, keeping the figure away from her. She aimed her car toward a large parked SUV and accelerated.

Beck plowed into the parked truck. The airbag smashed Beck in the face. She lay bleeding and unconscious. Jamal limped away from the scene before the couple got to Beck.

Sixteen

Kate shook her head nonstop. That was the first thing Beck saw from the emergency room gurney. It was freezing. Her head and hand hurt pulsed with pain.

"Damn Beck, you should see your stitches. Black and blue better be your favorite colors." Kate's quip didn't match the concern Beck could see in her face. A doctor entered. A very, young handsome doctor. He distracted Kate. Lust replaced concern in lightning speed. This relieved Beck. She decided she couldn't be dying, even Kate wouldn't abandon a dying friend for a cute doctor. "Okay Rebekkah, I've told the orderlies to move you upstairs to a real bed. You're the luckiest woman I've examined today."

"Wait, I'm not staying here. I want to go home." The sentence took all the energy she had.

"Your head was cracked like an egg. The MRI scan results are good but we need to observe you. Concussions are nothing to play with," he said.

"Doctor, whatever happened to my head, only improved it, I can't." She had to stop as pain seared through her temples.

"Besides your health, you may want to stay here to avoid speaking to the police. The only reason they haven't questioned you is my medical opinion that you're not in any shape to talk to them."

"Question me?"

"You had a single vehicle accident. I assured them we found no signs of alcohol or drugs, but your blood work is not in yet. So, do yourself and me a favor, take advantage of our lovely facilities. Wilder Agency told us to give you a private room. They will cover what your insurance doesn't."

"Beck, you were out a long time and you look like death warmed over. It's time you do the right thing," argued Kate.

Beck nodded slightly, any movement hurt. The doctor exited.

"Should I call Will?" asked Kate, thinking it was obvious she would.

Beck groaned. Kate knew that meant no. "Why not? Oh shit, tell me your weird thinking tomorrow, rest now. I'll get you out of here in the morning." Kate kissed Beck on her bruised cheek. The curtain billowed as she exited.

Beck was glad she was staying. She was shaken to the core but not just by the crash. She was disturbed that she was willing to kill them. Kill herself. She also was unnerved that Jamal, that fiendish prick, had been ordered to do what? Kill her, or just scare the holy shit out of her? When Beck saw him loom up in the backseat all she could think of was that Safra had invaded her space twice, and this time she was going to control it. She and Will had checked her phones for bugs, even got a device that swept the place for spyware. Now Safra had someone waiting for her in her car. She became scared all over again. She saw the outline of a figure behind the curtain. Finally, they were coming to get her and fill her with drugs. She could go into that death kind of sleep that doesn't allow for dreams, good or bad.

"Okay warden, take the prisoner. I'm ready to go." Beck closed her eyes.

Suddenly she felt a sharp agonizing pain shoot through her bandaged hand. What the hell was wrong with this orderly? She opened her eyes. Staring down at her were Safra's white blue eyes. Jamal was right behind him. He had a huge bandage over his right eye. Beck got a warm feeling from the blood that seeped onto the white cloth. Safra squeezed her hand.

"What's the matter? Too much pressure applied to a sensitive place? Such pain can be inflicted emotionally as well as physically. For example, when an innocent person is implicated in heinous acts, that implication creates pressure so severe it can ruin a person's life," he said coldly.

"The word innocent sounds obscene when you say it."

"I do admire you Rebekkah, it takes guts to smash your car into a non-moving object. Or maybe it's just another sign of an imminent mental breakdown, or maybe just a death wish, but that's the same thing." Safra eased his grip, slightly. Beck looked at Jamal when she spoke.

"Not crazy. I followed the rule to never let the creep take you from the place he attacks you because the second place will be a grave. I'd rather kill myself than let your hired psycho do it." Jamal wanted to smash her in the mouth. He lunged for her but Safra blocked him.

"Take it now," Safra commanded. Jamal held up his cell phone and took a picture of Safra holding Beck's hand. As soon as the camera flashed, they left.

Beck yelled after them. "Hey, Richard, who was Olivia going to marry?" Beck's heart pounded a mile a minute. What was that? Why the picture? The rings on the rod squealed when the curtain was drawn back. She released a blood curdling scream that caused the nurse to drop the medication that Beck so desperately wanted.

***

Beck was car sick. She rested her head next to the cool window pane. Kate's perfume was about to make her puke, but she didn't complain. She shouldn't have told her anything until they got home, but Kate was too good a reporter. Once Kate got one answer, she was relentless.

"A picture, what the hell for? You know the hospital has security cameras, why don't you complain?"

"Complain that my boss came to see me after I was in a terrible car wreck? That would put a nice pink bow on the Oldman's crazy box."

"Beck, this has gotten too dangerous. He's not just following you; he's trying to kill you. Twice in one day."

"The street thing was timed, a warning. The SUV was waiting for me. Jamal somehow signaled it. I don't think Safra wants me dead. If he did, I would be. In fact, I think it unnerved him that I crashed my car. It showed him that he can't control me. He still has plans for me, which keeps me alive. Enough about him. What do you think about my scheme?"

"Yeah a show about female circumcision is a good idea. I talked to Rachel from the Alliance, shit, way too much information for me. What about women doing that to women, what the hell?"

"After prosecuting sex crimes for years, it struck me how it wasn't enough to beat a woman, torture her, even murder her, she had to be raped too. Maybe if we were scraped out and looked like baby dolls, females would just be murdered."

Kate looked at Beck in the rear view mirror. "Umm Beck, are you feeling okay, we can always go back and see that cute doctor."

"What's going on Kate?"

Kate sighed, she hated what she knew. "The cops want to question you. Harvey had to get your car out of police impound. There's rumbling that you are behaving like you did during the LeMond case. The car crash is exhibit A. In fact, LeMond made a statement to the Press today. He mused on what made Wilder hire you in the first place and how sad it is that Safra has to suffer a missing child and finding her may be more difficult because of your being on the case. There's also word the cops may have someone of real interest for the murders. You're going to hate this, but gossip is that Will has been a hindrance too, that they could've gotten this guy weeks ago if Will had followed directives not to work with you."

Beck closed her eyes. She felt like Cassandra from the myths, telling truths that no one believed and cast her as insane.

"Safra is holding a news conference today, in just a few minutes actually. The Mayor will be there to kiss his feet. Safra's expected to stave off the gossip that you tried to commit suicide. So Machiavellian, he's going to express concern about the crash that he caused. I'm sure he'll throw a lot of money out to some political hacks while he's pretending to stand by you. People are feeling sorry for that creep."

All of this bad news perked Beck up. "If he's going so are all of his thugs. It's our chance to search Olivia's room. His place isn't far; we could be there in a few minutes."

Kate slowed the car down. "What do you mean we? This isn't an *I Love Lucy* episode. I'm not going."

Beck smiled. "Sure you are Ethel, you wouldn't miss it."

***

Kate whistled at the grandeur of the Safra estate. They waited patiently for someone to open the massive doors. Beck knew it would not do to have Jamal there but she wanted to kick him in the balls so bad that she would deal with the setback. Instead they were greeted by a very young African American man.

"May I help you," he asked.

"Yes, did Mr. Safra tell you to expect us? I'm Rebekkah Oldman and this is Kate Taylor. I am here to search Olivia Safra's room. As you can see I'm injured so Ms. Taylor is here to help me."

The young man's consternation was palatable. "I'm sorry, Mr. Safra did not tell me anything of the kind, and I am not able to bother him right now."

Beck spoke in a sympathetic tone. "What's your name?"

"Robert."

"Well Robert, what you may not know is that I work for Mr. Safra. I am a private investigator and I am trying to find Olivia Safra. I have gone beyond the call of duty to work today, to comply with Mr. Safra's instructions. If I don't do this now, I'm not sure when I can come back, and of course this will slow my progress."

Robert bit his lip as he weighed his options. He shook his head, "No, I'm sorry; he didn't convey any of this to me."

Beck couldn't believe she couldn't break this kid's resolve. Kate already started back to the car, relieved.

Beck began to sway. "Kate, help me."

Kate bounded up the steps, held onto Beck. "Kid, you got to let us in. She just got out of the hospital."

Robert reluctantly allowed the swooning woman into his boss's home. He took Beck's other arm and helped to seat her.

She spoke in a very weak voice. "May I please have some water and aspirin?"

Robert nodded nervously. When he was gone, Kate whispered to her.

"Beck, are you faking it?"

"No kidding." She whispered. She remained semi prostrate; she heard Robert's very fast approaching footsteps. Robert returned with water. He spoke defensively. "I cannot find a single aspirin. Maybe you should go to a drugstore now."

"Well how hard did you look, I mean you weren't gone very long," said Kate.

"I looked," he snapped

Beck saw that Kate made him defensive, scared, exactly the opposite response she needed. Beck looked at Kate helplessly. Kate got the message and gave Beck some water.

"Thank you. That helped. Robert, since I'm here and I don't want Mr. Safra angry with you, or me, why don't I call him. Of course that would interrupt his meeting with the Mayor, but if you need him to tell you to let me do my job, then that's what you need. Kate, could you hand me my phone?"

"No, don't. Fine, do it now," moaned Robert. Beck and Kate shot the look of success to each other. Beck didn't have to remind herself to move slowly, the fatigue and pain.

***

Beck and Kate were very impressed with the elevator. It had walnut panels, piped in music and a mini chandelier. When it stopped, Robert let them out into a huge hallway with about a million doors. They followed him for quite a while. He stood to the side. "This was Miss Safra's room."

"Was?" asked Beck.

"It's scheduled for a renovation. You may enter now."

Beck didn't move. "So she did use it?" He would not answer her.

"I thought you were in a hurry?" he asked impatiently.

"Robert, could I ask you again to get me some aspirin? It would help me speed up the process." Robert's disdain was evident, he wanted it to be. Beck motioned for Kate to give her the phone. Kate started to hand it to Beck but not before Robert quickly left.

They entered the room and were shocked, especially Kate. "Is this the broom closet? What's the point of having Daddy Warbucks as a father when he treats you like this?" Kate stood with her hands on her hips, disapproving.

It was small not just in comparison to the mansion but compared to any bedroom. As they walked down the hallway, they could see into luxury suites. Each had chandeliers and huge windows. This room was dark. The furniture was utilitarian. This was a mansion that the Queen of England would have been awed by, except for this room. The women looked at the room with disgust. "He can't stand her, Kate, I told you that. Works for us. Can you imagine if we had to search one of those suites?"

"What the hell am I looking for?" whined Kate.

Beck thumbed through the pages of a book. "Got me. It's like pornography, you'll know it when you see it."

"This is stupid. I don't know where to look for something that I have no clue what the something is."

"Improvise," chided Beck.

She was busy going through a chest of drawers. She found a small picture frame containing a photograph of a beautiful African woman with almond eyes, dark satin skin, and winter white teeth. Sitting next to her was a young girl, her replica; the only difference was the girl's skin was the color of light coffee. They wore identical rings of huge black stones wrapped in silver rope. Beck took the picture out of the frame, stuffed it into her pocket.

Kate was on her hands and knees, she yanked sheets from their corners and felt under the mattress. She pulled out an artist sketch-pad. Beck saw the door move slightly and hobbled to it. No one, she looked down the hallway. She saw someone round a corner, she was sure it was Robert. It was time to get the hell out of there. "Hey Kate, I think Robert was watching us."

Kate tucked the pad under her loose shirt. "That's it. We're doing some form of burglary. You're a lawyer knowingly committing a felony. We're poking the monster in his eye. Safra's going to know what we did. I want to leave, now. Now, Beck."

Kate led the way to the elevator. Robert met them with the aspirin. This shocked Beck, she couldn't have seen Robert only moments ago. Who the hell was it? Her head was pounding. She decided not to tell Kate that she didn't actually see Robert and she suspected Safra's thugs saw them. How to get out of there fast? She pretended to feel light headed. That was the last thing

Robert needed. "Let's go down to the kitchen, it will get you to your car faster," he whimpered fearfully. Kate smiled as the doors closed.

Seventeen

The soft music, six aspirin, and one bottle of beer did a lot to dull Beck's throbbing body and mind. After Kate helped check the apartment, both of them armed with pepper spray, she took a hot shower, put on her favorite pajamas and allowed herself to rest. No computers, no phones, no TV. She even let Kate buy her a hot meal of chicken, vegetables, potatoes, hot tea, and cookies. Good ol' Kate. She looked about as beat as Beck when she left. Well-fed, well-medicated, and calmer than she had been for what seemed a century, Beck looked at the picture she took from Olivia's drawer. The thin frame had been jammed in a space of wood that was coming loose. She almost missed it. She reached for the artist pad when the phone rang. Shit, she forgot to turn off the landline.

Will spoke after the beep. "Please listen, Beck. Don't disconnect. There's a lot of shit being spread about you staging the accident. I don't know if you saw or heard Safra's conference today, his phony support of you was disgusting. They're working up a case against Tommy Justin. No, they're manufacturing. Please, let me see you. I hate that you didn't call me when you were in the hospital, but why would you? I was a prick. Beck?"

With Herculean effort she pulled her aching body from the sofa to the landline.

"Ten minutes. I'm going to bed in a half an hour." She hung up. Before she could take three steps the phone rang again. She didn't care who it was, she hobbled slowly to the sofa.

"Beck, you are fired." Harvey's voice reverberated through the answering machine. "Did you really, really go in his house? Have you heard what's being said about you, Blake, me? If you survive the fall that he has cooking up, you can put yourself right next to Jesus as a miraculous resurrection. He used us. I don't know what he did or is doing but I'm sorry Beck, sorry I got you into this. Take my advice; get the hell out of here, fast and far. No one has anything on you; you're cleared on the car thing. Did he do that to you, Beck? And Blake, take the kid with you. Safra's got him twisted up too. Guess he may be listening to this, but at this point, I don't give a shit. Bye Beck, I'll see you after I come back from a long trip, after you come back from a longer one."

Harvey had a difficult time hanging up the phone. Was he drunk or scared to death?

Beck was terrified, but as usual, her friend anger took over. She was furious that everyone was being destroyed by Safra. She noticed the pad again, made it to the sofa. She grabbed it roughly like if she hurt it somehow the pain would transfer to Safra. The first pages were sketches of women, girls, mostly nudes. Typical first sketches if Olivia had been an art student, but she wasn't. The next pages were renderings of women without mouths. The sketches were ghoulish. She was disturbed by them and by the knock on the door.

Beck looked through the peephole, opened the door. When Will saw her injuries, tears welled-up in his eyes. He wanted to hold her, she wanted him to hold her, but the scene in the bar had created a barrier so all he could muster was, "Jesus Beck."

She let him get the beer and the glasses. They sat together on the sofa but not too close. Her look demanded that he speak. He obeyed. "All of a sudden a ton of evidence is appearing in a case that had not a scintilla. All of it points to Tommy. His clothes have hairs and blood from the victims. The same forensics have been found in his car. A black sedan, by the way. It doesn't matter that it's old, beat up, peeling paint, or that it looks more grey than black. Here's the best part: Tommy, the serial killer, has vanished, from the police station."

"What do you mean vanished?" she asked incredulously

"I mean poof, Tommy is no longer in custody. No one knows how he could have escaped from a room full of armed and trigger happy cops. This is very hush-hush. Ostensibly for the good of the public. He's supposed to be a serial killer but it's to be kept quiet? No warnings to the public that he's on the loose? Why aren't pictures of him plastered everywhere? Because it is all total and complete bullshit. Oh, and my own personal bonus is that I have been kicked off the case."

The throbbing in Beck's head began again. "Why? I mean what made this happen now?"

"I think I have the link that connects the girls." Will relished the moment. He wanted her to have to ask him what. She complied. "What link? What is it?" she asked excitedly.

"After to talking to a lot of people, it became clear that all of these girls had been sexually active or around sex in some perverse way. All except Ella, she's still not making sense to me. Tamara is the product of rape. Camille, as we know was sexually active, the source of fighting with her grandmother but the fighting wasn't just about sex, it was the fact Camille was having sex with her first cousins. There's a nice family photo. Jasmine's mother was a prostitute. Erica has had three, count them, three pregnancies. And here's the kicker, they all went to the same free clinic, one near the university. All of the girls, Jasmine's mother, Camille, her grandmother, everyone got care there like birth control, abortion counseling. The white offerings make sense, the calling back of childhood and innocence. Not that bullshit white racist interpretation. These girls had their innocence taken from them. See, reading poetry is a practical skill."

"So you crack the code and they kick you off the case? That's about right," she intoned derisively.

"I told all of this to the Lieutenant, and I told him about another link." He waited again.

"Shit, Will, why do I have to ask?" she blurted. "Safra, I said, is involved," he announced. Beck wanted to kiss the shit out of him but all she could muster was, "Fuck." He smiled.

"That's exactly what the Lieutenant said. Suddenly I'm assigned other cases, mostly confined to my desk. Within the hour I was sent an email, mind you, an email that I was on temporary suspension because a complaint had been made against me. Total bullshit. A complaint with no formal paperwork, or they can't show it to me for review? That's against every last union rule. Someone very high in the food chain pulled my plug."

"They believe it's true, Will. They know you know Tommy is being set-up. That makes you a dangerous person and that's dangerous for them. What made you change your mind about Safra?" she asked in an "I told you so" tone.

"I hadn't changed my mind. It was a test for them and for me. If they tweaked when I said Safra, then there had to be something to his involvement. If nothing else he's directing them to set up Tommy, but why if he wasn't involved? It started to make some sense. His hiding Olivia's pending marriage really bugged me. I tried to find out about that, got nothing, not a word but I believe the Ibish kid. He had his daughter set up for an arranged marriage that went bad. Safra has enough juice to steer the investigation. He is the sugar daddy to the department and the Mayor."

"Well, while you were put on temporary suspension, Harvey fired me." Now it was Beck's turn to make him ask.

"For what reason?" Will was surprised.

"He's afraid. He said Safra is after us. Clearly from what you just said, he's right. He said to get out of town for a while. Safra's plan is working. I'm a crazy bitch who ran her car into a parked SUV. You have been corrupted by me. Safra's been damaged by our ineptitude. His daughter is still missing and now a serial killer has escaped, even though no one knows that."

"Kate told me that Safra's guy was hiding in the backseat of your car. Maybe Harvey's right, maybe it's time to get the hell out," he said.

"You're off the case. I'm fired. Tommy is set-up. If we stay involved, we could be brought up on some phony obstruction charge. So far working with me has only cost you your job and your reputation. You want it to cost your freedom?" asked Beck.

Will moved next to Beck, he embraced her very gently. "I want to be with you. You have make me feel good about myself, comfortable in my own skin. I admire your strength; you stand up for what you know is right. Granted, you do have issues, stealing not the least of them, you're a slob, and you get pissed off really easily but all in all…"

Beck kissed him passionately. She had missed him. She was exhausted and realized she wanted, even needed Will's presence. She and Safra were in some kind of death match; she still didn't know her role. Will held her tightly. "I'm not quitting, Will, not until I show Safra to be the monster I know he is. I may be going down that rabbit hole, and I know he'll come down after me."

"Then we need to make the most of our time, Alice." Will was careful with her arm as he took off her pajamas.

***

A lone ray of sunshine infiltrated its way into the bedroom. Beck negligently had not battened down the window shades completely. Will slept deeply next to her. She leaned against the headboard, used her knees as a desk as she thumbed through Olivia's sketches. "Will, Will, wake up." She shook him. He was very groggy, slow to realize where he was. "What time is it?" he asked.

"I found something, or actually Kate found it." He did not respond. Beck shoved him, roughly. "Jesus Beck, what?" She patted his back as an apology.

"Okay when we were at the estate, Kate found this artist pad under the mattress. She clearly thought she was going back there because she left this and some other things, but Daddy had other plans, including a room renovation. He knew she was never returning, Will, because dead people can't have a sleepover."

Will worked to be alert. She gave him the pad. He looked through the nudes, then the nudes without mouths, then women missing parts of their breasts. The women's upper bodies were voluptuous, but below the waist the legs were stick figures, like a child would draw.

"God, she drew these?" Beck nodded, pointed to the O.S., signed on each page. She took the pad back. "O.S. Olivia Safra. She wrote something on the back of the sketches."

Will scrunched down into the covers. This annoyed Beck. "Are you listening?" She realized she needed to calm down. She cleared her throat to make sure Will was listening. "It wasn't enough what was done to me when I was five years old. I can still see the old, blue veined-hands digging into the flesh on my wrists, burying my strength into the dirt. That wrinkled face rising up from between my legs, the dirty nails cutting into my thighs. The curled fingers that clenched the shards of glass. Then the fire, the white heat blazed up my thighs into my gut. I could smell the metal of my own blood and it caused me to wretch. His eyes will not look into mine; he says I am not clean enough. What he doesn't know is that pain seared hatred of my own body. Now I must do more to be pure for the marriage. He will love me then."

Beck stopped reading. They felt embarrassed, like voyeurs. Olivia was to be pitied, and mourned.

Beck looked at each page. "Look, this was written one week before she was reported missing. She died to please Daddy. This is evidence of what he was doing to her, how he felt about her. You know he won't rest until he's sure there's nothing that can connect him to this. This could destroy him. Will, you have to think Tommy is dead. He will be found with a treasure trove of evidence driving the nail into his new coffin. Then Olivia's body will be found, another one of his kills." Will agreed. "And her blood will be added to the ironclad case against him. The salient fact that Olivia has been dead for God knows how long will never come out in the ME'S report. The End." Will's tone was suppressed anger.

Will put on his jeans, went to the window. He reminded Beck of how a prisoner gazes out of his cell window. "No, not the end, the beginning. Will, meet me at the news station at four. Kate and I already have something cooking and it could just be another way to end this tale."

"Last time you were on TV you, well you know. Are you sure you want to go to the public?" he asked.

Beck jumped out of bed, put her arms around his waist. "I'm not going to the public Will, I'm going to Safra."

Eighteen

Rachel could not have been more pleased when she was called by Kate Taylor to do a short segment on female circumcision. It was a practice that needed to be brought to light. Her nose had been powdered for what seemed the millionth time. The lights were intense, and she never did cool off from the muggy heat outside. She was ready for the cue from the director. Kate let her know generalities but did not prep her on specific questions. She didn't want Rachel to think that there was a script. She was glad Beck Oldman was there but wasn't sure what her purpose was. So far it was going very well.

Kate nodded affirmatively. "Thank you Rachel. I think that clearly sets up the philosophy behind the practice. So now more about the procedure itself. I understand there can be very severe cutting. If it isn't done by a doctor, or even if it's done by a doctor, is there concern of something going wrong?"

"The cutting you refer to is called infibulation. Yes, of course there is concern with an invasive procedure to the body. There can be extreme loss of blood, shock, infections can lead to death, but that is very rare," Rachel said with authority.

"If this is something that is done traditionally, underground as you referred to it, then there's a good chance these girls would not get needed medical attention," Kate added anxiously.

"Yes, unfortunately people who immigrate to this country for example, and do the procedure are afraid to take their daughters to the hospital, afraid of being charged with abuse and losing child custody. Remember, this is not designed to be abusive. They love their daughters."

"Ms. Oldman was on the show a few weeks ago. Thank you for returning. You're a private investigator for Wilder Agency hired to find Olivia Safra. Since you were on last time, you think you have found a link between this practice of female circumcision and the disappearance of Ms. Safra?"

Beck was dressed in a black blazer and white crisp blouse. Her silver earrings sparkled. She was effervescent, her cheeks filled with blood. She was on the hunt and it made her sharp. She was careful not to be too energetic; she had to be the picture of perfect mental health even though she was riding a tornado.

"I did work for the Wilder Agency, but have recently been fired," she answered in a matter-of-fact tone.

Kate gasped. Beck withheld that bombshell from Kate; she didn't it want to cloud the issue. Kate knew if she asked anything about the firing, the focus on circumcision would be lost. She let Beck continue. "I met Rachel while I was still working for the agency. Shortly after, I found out that Olivia Safra was to undergo infibulation and that this was to be her second circumcision. This was to occur about one week before her disappearance. Rachel, even though she is an adult, would this be kept from her father if she were a devout Muslim and believed in traditional roles between daughter and father?"

Rachel was taken aback, where was this going? "Well, I don't know Ms. Safra. Typically the family is involved. If she was of age and she were doing this let's say because she was going to be married, then I would guess, just guess, that her father would be involved. A rich family like hers could provide excellent medical care, too."

Beck couldn't have been happier. Okay Kate, she thought, ask the question. Rachel set it up for you.

"Was she? Was Olivia Safra engaged?" gasped Kate. Beck looked directly in the camera, directly at Safra when she answered.

"Yes, it seems so. Strange we know nothing about who this man is or when the marriage was to take place. There are a lot of secrets around this dangerous operation too. Did she have it? Did something go wrong? There are secrets about Olivia's life that were withheld from me, and worse from the police with whom shall we say, Mr. Safra has a very special relationship. I hope he is more forthcoming with critical information to help solve the mystery of his daughter's disappearance. She is a devout Muslim who honors her faith and is obedient to her father."

The director cued Kate to wrap. Kate knew that this time Beck's appearance wasn't going to end with just a scolding. She dropped a bomb that was going to explode. When Kate looked into the camera, it crossed her mind that it might be for the last time.

"If you have any questions for Rachel at the Woman's Alliance, please use the number on the screen. I want to thank my guests and wish you a goodnight."

Kate was calm, not Rachel. "I came on this show to educate people, not to set up circumcision as a murder weapon. You have caused so much damage. You just gave people a reason to go deeper underground. And how it was left with the focus on Muslims? I told you other religions practice circumcision on females. I am sure the only thing anyone will remember from this so-called educational spot will be that Olivia Safra's father did something to her and that all Muslims butcher their daughters. Using me like you did is rude. Using girls who are victims, that's criminal. I hope you get what you want. And I thought Safra was sleazy."

Rachel stormed toward the director with whom she had a few choice words to share. He was already being skewered on the phone. After Rachel blasted him, he screamed at Kate. "Your friend just cost us our jobs."

Beck ran over to him. "Why? I'm the only one who talked about Safra?" He looked at Beck with disgust. "You said it on her show, our show. Rachel was right, you used all of us. He left, beaten.

"I knew what I was doing, Beck," Kate said. "We were going to lift the lid on Pandora's Box. Safra must have called the owner of the station the second he saw you. We knew he'd hit hard. Oh, there's Will, late again. I'll call you later." Kate hugged Beck. She was in no hurry to go upstairs and hear the official word.

Will walked briskly toward Beck, clutching a brown envelope. Beck looked to him to ease the guilt that she felt, but it was second to her feelings of excitement that something was about to break.

Will spoke first. "Beck, they found Erica Hubbard, her body was discovered at a preschool playground. We may have a lead, the bumper sticker has been traced to a small rental agency. It's in a rural town I never heard of, McKinley. It's about seventy some miles from here. The rental agency is small but they still have a surveillance camera. There's a picture of their logo on the wall, it matches the piece of the bumper sticker." Will took out a photograph from the envelope. It showed the company logo and an agent behind a counter waiting on customers. Two of the customers had on baseball caps. Then she saw it. She opened her mouth a couple of times but no words came out. She pointed at the men in the picture. Will looked. "Yeah, I know, guys in baseball hats, but the rental company manager said they've had no suspicious rentals," he responded.

Beck poked the photograph so hard she almost put a hole in it. "No, no look. See that ring? I have a picture of Olivia and her mother wearing identical rings. That ring. The ring that's on that guy's hand." Will snatched the picture from her.

"It's Olivia's ring. Did that bastard pay the killer with his daughter's ring? Did the killer take it off of her dead body? We've got to find this guy, Will. He's the killer and he's the proof she's dead."

Will walked in small circles. He was in his detective clothes; his tie felt like it was choking him. "We have to go to McKinley, Will, now," Beck commanded.

Will's phone rang. She shook her head for him not to answer. He ignored her, turned his back to take the call. When he finished, he spoke to her sternly. "You have to go home. Straight home Beck, no detours. I have to go back to work. I will come to your place as soon as I can, but you promise me, go home and wait for me."

"Yeah, but Will…"

"No, Beck, no but's. You have to go home and stay there. I have to go. I was given a direct order. The dam is breaking, Beck, things are shifting really fast. Don't do anything except wait for me. You promise?"

She nodded. They clung to each other wondering what the hell was next.

***

Wrath was a sin that Safra cultivated. He embraced it and knew how to exact its power against his enemies. The TV glowed in the background. Again Beck's face dominated the huge theatre screen. Her silver earrings did indeed sparkle. He waited patiently. Ahh, there, the phone, he answered. "Yes, now, it's time. Are they in place? When I call you, that's when. Yes, finally."

***

Harvey was stone cold sober and he couldn't figure out how. He had lost count of how many scotches he threw back at the bar but he could still walk a straight line to his car. It had been years since he graced the old cop bar. Not since he started to don thousand dollar suits and affected smoking cigars with other CEOs. There wasn't a single familiar back to slap or face to give him some solace on the day he suffered his own personal holocaust. The rain finally stopped for a few minutes. What a bitch of a summer, it had been nothing but a wet stinking sauna. Days filled with dead girls and a feeling he was not accustomed to, fear. Why did that bastard insist on hiring Beck? He tried to tell him that Beck wouldn't let go, she had more balls than the entire NFL. The fact that she was small and half-demented didn't stop her from pursuing what she thought was right. When he looked up at the blinding lights and heard the squealing tires on wet pavement, Harvey was smiling. His body did at least two full rotations in the air before it bounced and splattered on the pavement. The last sound he made on this earth was the gurgling of blood in his mouth, blood mixed with scotch. The last thing Harvey saw was his blood flow into a dirty puddle, turning it a crimson black.

Nineteen

Beck slept sprawled across her bed. Her head was bent to the side; drool seeped out of the corner of her mouth. She drank successfully that night. She got the affect that had eluded Harvey. Her senses had been dulled by the beer. Her mind was calmed from the hundreds of dollars spent on TV shopping. The credit card lay on her chest. The cell phone cast a green light before it rang. It rang but didn't awaken her. The caller tried again, this time she woke up. The thought of Will overcame the beer's sedation.

"Will, where the hell are you?"

"Ms. Oldman?" asked a woman's voice. "I have information for you, Ms. Oldman, crucial information."

Beck sat up, her head throbbed. It was one in the morning. Did someone die? Where's Will? Will. The woman spoke again, in a weird, sing song, childlike voice.

"Of course I know it's you, Ms. Oldman, and you know who I am. Answer me, or I will hang up." Beck inhaled deeply, she felt faint. She was determined to sound coherent. "I know you're someone who works for Safra. Where's Jamal, hiding in the back of a school bus?"

The woman laughed derisively.

"Ms. Oldman, let's not play games. I saw you in my room at the estate. It turns out I have no more patience than my father. You work for him, so you know what that means. If you want answers, then you will meet me in exactly two and a half hours at

1422 Belmont Street, in McKinley. I know you're familiar with the town. I will be waiting for exactly two hours and forty five minutes. That should give you time to get to that car of yours. By the way, you parked across from the flower shop."

"Hey, hello, hello, talk to me?" Beck asked a dead connection.

Beck wasn't sure if she was really awake. She turned on the light. Okay, yes awake. She didn't believe that was Olivia, she was dead. Beck smelled a trap a mile away. She had to call Will. "No, I've done enough to him," she said aloud. Beck checked her backpack for pepper spray. Typed on the computer. Pressed the print button. Shit, she should have let Harvey teach her how to use the phone's GPS. She'd tell him that. She owed him one "I told you so." She was out of the apartment in five minutes. She was glad that bitch whoever she is knew where Beck had parked her car.

**

Beck only got lost only once. Driving fast was one of her favorite things to do and now as she sat on Belmont Street, alone and unarmed, she wished she had driven more slowly. The tree-lined suburban street glistened from the soft rain. There were few houses near the burnt out Mosque. Its skeleton stood tall. A victim of a violent crime. Beck remembered reading about the violence that the good people of McKinley exacted against the small, peaceful Muslim community after 9/11. The racism infuriated her and the allusion that she was a bigot by Rachel stung hard. She had to make the point of Muslim's practicing circumcision to lure out Safra. Beck would have to take on the persona of Scarlett O'Hara and think about the damage she may have caused tomorrow. A wind began to pick up and the branches of the trees seemed to be reaching out for her. Instead of a welcoming cathedral, she felt entrapped. Her brain told her to get out of there. Her stubbornness ordered her to check her backpack and get her ass out of the car.

There was obscene graffiti against Muslims sprayed painted on the scarred building. She walked to the front entrance. One door hung off its hinges. She got a small flash light from her pack and entered, always looking over her shoulder. It didn't smell of smoke or char. The thick, sickly odor of mildew took over. There had been no attempt to resurrect the Mosque. Shards of glass lay where they landed over a decade ago. She had to walk carefully through the landmine of debris. Old fixtures and stingy wires hung from the skeletal walls. In spite of the rain a few thin rays of moonlight came through, casting distorted shadows.

A thud of something falling resonated throughout the eerie structure. It was followed by the squealing of a rat. Beck jumped back. She lost her footing and tripped over of a piece of wood and fell face down. Her flashlight was thrown out of her hands. She was hurt. There wasn't enough moonlight to help her find her flashlight or regain her footing. There was no one there. She knew she was on a wild goose chase, or worse, a set up. She should call Will. He was going to be furious that she didn't follow his adamant pleas to stay at the apartment. She felt something warm flowing down her lip. She hated to do it, in case the rat or its friends were close but she searched through the trash to find the flashlight. She lucked out, turned it on. The first thing she saw was blood on her fingers. Her face was bleeding. She aimed the light near her feet to be sure there were was nothing to trip over or step on. Beck gathered herself to get the hell out of there, but found herself face to face with a tall figure, dressed in a black gown, and a torn veil that covered the entire face.

Beck cried out. She fell backwards but struggled not to go down again. She pointed the weak light on the figure. The only sound or movement was the squealing and scattering of the vermin in the trash. Slowly, the veil was lifted, exposing a gaunt face, hollowed eye sockets, and grayish skin that looked as if it were covered in ash. Beck frantically searched for the pepper spray and her phone. Beck felt she was facing the Grim Reaper.

"Finally, Ms. Oldman, we meet in this once holy place. A place burned down by ignorance and prejudice. The town needed to cleanse itself from people of my faith. Innocent people who loved this country and were victims of that terrible day too, but I understand the need to cleanse, to purify. The town was successful. I think I am the only Muslim here and I'm just a traveler. Do you see me? Do you see that you were wrong? I am not murdered by my father."

Beck's mind raced. Was this really Olivia? Then why would Safra kill those girls? Did he? Shit, what had she done? How could she have been so wrong? Had she hounded him for nothing? No, no, there's something she hadn't seen, and Olivia had to tell her.

"Those girls were murdered. He's involved. Did he try to kill you? That's a death sentence for you. It's just a matter of time before he finds you." Finds her. Beck was hired to find Olivia so he could kill her. But why? How do Jasmine and the other girls figure in? Her mind raced until she realized that he probably followed her. They had to get out if they wanted to live. Olivia laughed in staccato notes. It unnerved Beck.

"You are so lost. Those girls are my sisters. We share African blood. They, and only they are worthy to be pure and eternal, to be liberated from their sordid lives. I even removed their fingertips so there's no identity to their pasts."

Shit, shit she had it backwards: she did it, Olivia was the killer. Beck felt waves of emotion. The first one was shock. Wave two violence. She wanted to kill the crazy bitch in front of her.

"How could my father ever think you were so brilliant, held such insight, when you can't see what's in front of you, even now," Olivia said in that sick little girl voice, a voice that belied the specter in front of Beck.

Wave three, nausea. Safra hired her to find Olivia to stop her from butchering another kid. Beck's legs gave out; she squatted, head between her knees. When she looked up, Olivia held a gun on her. She aimed it directly at Beck's head. She handled it skillfully. Beck decided the best tactic was to ignore the weapon and to try and make Olivia talk.

"Why, why, did you do this? Why did you kill those girls?" pleaded Beck. She had to know why they died but she had to know fast. If Safra followed her, he couldn't be far away.

Olivia seemed disconnected to the moment; she looked around, up, down. She moved as if she were floating. Her voice lost the child tone, the singsong remained but now it was eerie. It didn't sound like it came from her body. "Their pain was my pain. It had to be done. I watched many girls get cut in Africa. After it was done to me, I became obsessed, had to watch it being done. The village encouraged girls to watch other girls being purified. There was always so much blood, so much screaming. I learned enough in my medical training to make sure they wouldn't suffer like I had."

"You murdered and mutilated painlessly?" asked Beck. Olivia didn't seem to hear her. She had to keep her talking. Maybe Beck could get the gun before Safra slaughtered both of them.

"They needed honor. I understood because I needed honor, I had lost it. I had lost it for my father. I can't have children. I was torn to shreds in Africa. The one chance I had for my father to accept me as his child was the marriage he arranged. He recognized my existence enough to find a suitable husband, a rich man whose family could align with ours, but the man demanded a circumcision. I thought I could blame my barrenness on this circumcision. Give me time to cement the alliance, get my father to--I demanded that we used a traditional practitioner, a woman. I allowed the doctor to be present. I set up the woman to take the blame that my father would not have a grandson. The chance of his having a grandson was as much motivation to accept me as the power alliance. The woman told the doctor, after she performed the infibulation, of the previous damage. She said I would never bear a child. The world caved in around me. After the doctor confirmed her report I was shunned, cursed, called a liar and a cheat. In some countries I would have been killed by the man who was to marry me. He spit on me in front of my father. That was the last time I saw him. I would venture it was the last time anyone saw him. The marriage was a business alliance. My lie and the disappearance of my betrothed cost my father millions of dollars, and gave the man's family leverage over him. Worse, it brought him shame. I dishonored him. I tried to play him, isn't that the term? I was dead to him, forever."

"They mutilated you Olivia. They whittled your body like it was a piece of wood. Honor? Where was any honor for you? Fuck honor, did you ever get a second of love since your mother died? Did your father ever treat you like a human being? If you had been born with a penis Olivia, and were infertile, they would have blamed or killed a woman because of it. Jesus, all of those girls died because of what? I still don't know." Olivia cocked her head as Beck raged against what Olivia had suffered. No one had ever done that for her before. For a moment she forgot about the gun. Beck tried to move closer to her, but Olivia adjusted her hold and aim.

"You murdered girls so the man who won't say your name, or call you his daughter would love you? Only the daughter of Richard Safra could think slaughtering innocent children could earn brownie points."

"It wasn't slaughter, don't you say that again. Look at their lives. I volunteered at the clinic. It was such a cesspool. They never checked my fake ID. That's where I saw Jasmine's mother constantly getting AIDS and STD tests. Camille flaunted sex with her relatives. All of them were unclean and damned to a life of pimps, drugs, poverty, and abuse. I got to know them, befriended them. I told Jasmine about her mother, she had been lied to. I gave them comfort and I promised each of them that I would come and get them and save them from the sordidness. I gave them eternal bliss and honor."

"Honor, bliss? You murdered them. Jasmine was a happy kid whose father adored her; you brought the dirt into her life. You made her unclean, you stupid..." Beck couldn't stop the fourth wave: pure rage.

"Stupid? You would have never found me. I have money, access, skill with technology. I paid people to rent the cars. My father's indifference to me and my own dislike of photographs worked well. No one questioned my identity. You know he created an easy to access portal into your and Detective Blake's phones and computers. When the detective learned about McKinley, and you had that picture, I knew you would recognize the ring. I asked the man to wear it. I had to give a little clue. I knew you had taken the picture of my mother and me. You also violate privacy, Ms. Oldman. You've tainted the one thing I had of my mother's. Now it's yours." Olivia dug into her gown. She held up the ring. She motioned with the gun for Beck to move closer. "If you think you can take this gun from me, it will be your last thought. Hold out your hand." Beck complied. Olivia dropped the ring into Beck's hand.

A huge clap of thunder startled them. Olivia almost dropped the gun. A streak of lightning under the clouds made the scene even more ghoulish. She had to get the damn gun. "Your father knew you murdered the girls and he hired me to stop you," taunted Beck.

"Yes, I told him. I needed to make amends. I mailed a letter from a different state. If anyone found it, it wouldn't have made sense. It was typed and unsigned. Isn't he brilliant?" He hired a thief, a dishonored woman to find another dishonored woman. He knew that no matter what you found, no one would believe you. He made sure of it. His pretense of concern about me was the most care I had ever known."

"Then why the gun, Olivia, if no one will believe me?" Olivia looked down at her hand somewhat surprised by what she held. She kept looking for something.

"Because of what you did tonight, on the TV. You've set a wounded animal hunting. You took control from him tonight. This has to end now. You have to know that I had nothing to do with Ella. Ella was killed because you and Detective Blake led him to her. I don't understand why he killed her. I want him to be proud of me with this one last gift. You."

Beck exploded. "He killed Ella to kill you. You're next. No one will know Ella wasn't mutilated because he'll make sure of it. All you did with this carnage is make him hate you to death, Olivia."

A slash of lightning lit them up like a sound stage. Wind screamed through the broken walls and roof. Olivia became focused. Beck thought she was staring at her.

"I got her here for you." The child's voice returned. Jamal stepped out of the shadows behind Olivia, twisted her arm. The gun dropped easily.

Beck knew the presence behind her was Safra, she stuffed the ring into her back pocket. He walked to his daughter. Light was not needed to see that his face emanated seething hatred. His voice cracked with vile contempt. "From the moment of your birth you have been nothing but a massive disappointment to me. And now you tried to ruin me with your insanity. Your female neediness and disorganized thinking. No son would stoop to your level of degradation."

Olivia fell to her knees, she bent to kiss his feet, or so it looked to Beck. She was a crazy murderer but she had been turned into that by her bloodless bastard of a father. Beck couldn't bear to see her grovel at the monster's feet. She lunged to stop her but Jamal put the gun to Olivia's temple.

"Fucking bastard." Beck spoke in a flat tone. It was a statement of fact. She stood next to Jamal. She wished she had killed him in the crash. It was like he read her thought because he trained the gun from Olivia to Beck. Safra put his hand on her shoulders. His eyes were blank. "Rebekkah, you have not been a disappointment, not for a moment. You did everything I hoped. Everything Harvey promised, your guts, your tenacity, your self-destructiveness came through. We are a good team. You and I stopped her. I am sorry our partnership has come to an end." There was a slight sound of remorse in his voice.

This enraged Olivia. "How can you say those things to her? I am your daughter," she wailed. She reached out to her father. Her thin arms protruding out of the black gown was like death reaching for a victim. Beck struggled to get away but Jamal pushed her to the ground. He jerked her to her knees and stood behind her with the gun touching the back of her head.

It is like they say, Beck thought as she felt the explosion to her temple. Death comes quietly.

****

She pumped her legs as hard as she could and leaned back into the swing. She pointed her feet to the sky, admiring the crimson toes of the stiletto heels. The black robe trailed behind as the swing went up and back. She pumped harder for more air time. Beck, Jasmine, Camille, and Tamara swung in unison on swings next to hers. Their robes were slashed and splattered with streaks of red, the color of Beck's shoes.

Beck's suddenly was being pushed by a tall figure from behind, also dressed in black gown but the figure's face was covered by a ripped veil. As the arms pushed Beck, they seemed to grow in length meeting her sooner each time. Beck wanted to swing by herself. She was angry at the interference. The figure moved. Did it sense her agitation? It moved behind Camille who suddenly flew off the swing. Then each girl, except Jasmine flew off her swing and landed in the sandbox. They landed near where Ella was digging. Each scoop of sand was wet and red.

Beck swung so high she could see over the bar of the swing set. Her gown ripped from the velocity of the wind. The chains trembled. Then Jasmine sailed off and into the sandbox. Beck felt hands on her back. She was pushed hard by the figure in black and catapulted off the swing. She sailed feet first toward the girls. Her stiletto heels impaled Jasmine's jersey. Ninety-one took a direct hit. Beck started screaming. Jasmine sat up, unscathed by the high heels sticking in her chest. The girls were covered in blood. They waved bloody hands, fingertips missing, signaling Beck to join them. She tried to move but she was sinking in the red quicksand. The girls threw her kisses as she slowly disappeared. She smiled and called out, "Gloria. Look, Gloria, I did it. I saved my kids and I did it in high heels, just like you."

Twenty

Beck slashed at the air, struggled to disentangle herself from the sheet and blanket on her bed. She sat up like the girl in *The Exorcist*, straight up from the waist. Where was she? Why did she feel like she had been swinging? A nightmare that made her nauseous. Olivia, she was with her. Was that a nightmare too? She needed to throw up. Beck barely got to the toilet on time. She ran the cold water on her hands and saw it, Olivia's ring. She had on Olivia's ring. She vaguely remembered that it had been in her pocket, but she wasn't sure about anything. Why was she filthy? She started to shake. More cold water that would help. The water turned the blood into a red stream that trickled down her cheek. Shit, it wasn't a nightmare, these were fresh wounds. Someone brought her back to her apartment. Her home had been violated again. It was coming back to her. She thought she was being murdered by Jamal, but he must have just slugged her with the gun. What about Olivia? She yanked the ring off, it fell on the floor. When she picked it up, she saw that one of her feet was missing a sock and sneaker. Why did she expect to see a high heel on her foot? She stuffed the ring in her pocket. The landline phone rang. Will's voice was on the answering machine before she could hobble to the phone.

"Where are you? I've been trying you for hours. Why the hell is your cell...?"

"Will," she cut him off. Her voice was thick. "Will, Olivia."

"Are you talking about what's on TV? Where have you been? I told you not to leave. I'm on my way there." He hung up. He was more than just angry.

Beck decided she should leave the door open for him, she could barely walk and she was sick of being afraid and in constant lockdown. She turned on the TV looking for something that would match his message. Then she found it. A group of reporters stood in front of the gates of the Safra estate. A reporter was being cued to speak. He balked. Was this his first job? They will be sorry they fired Kate. Finally the novice spoke. "It's been reported that Olivia Safra's body was found in the basement of the apartment complex where Tommy Justin lived. Justin, a convicted felon, self-proclaimed white supremacist, and convicted sex offender was the prime suspect in the murder of five African American girls. Olivia Safra was shot in the head. We've been told, off the record, that she has been dead for weeks. Her body was found in a freezer. Ms. Safra has been the subject of an ongoing missing person's investigation. It is also reported that Justin's body was found in his apartment. His death is being called an apparent suicide caused by a single gunshot wound to his head. The same caliber of gun was used to kill Ms. Safra."

Beck turned off the sound. She felt empty. Will announced his arrival. He gasped when he saw her. She was equally upset by his haggard appearance. He looked as if he had aged overnight. It was probably the lighting but she thought she saw strands of silver in his black hair. They locked bloodshot eyes.

"What happened?" he asked first. "Will, did you see my car outside?" He nodded. Before she continued, he pointed to the TV. The crawl read that Safra was going to make a statement from City Hall that afternoon. Beck clicked the TV off. "I was with Olivia last night. The woman they just said has been dead for a long time. Freezer, good move, very good move."

Will slumped onto the sofa. He readied himself for what he knew was going to be more hellish information.

"She told me that she was the killer. She killed every last one of them, oh, no, wait, she didn't kill Ella, she was very clear about that."

Beck stood in front of Will, she was unsteady. "But then I killed Jasmine, when I was on the swing. I told you her death was my fault."

Will felt like he was under water, struggling to surface. "Beck, you've been hurt again. You've just survived a car wreck. You have to slow down. You did not kill Jasmine, and you were not on a swing last night, but I think you're right about Olivia. What did she say? How did you find her? Where were you?"

"McKinley. She hid there, in plain sight because no one knew what she looked like. She was, and I say this possessing intimate familiarity with the state, crazy. She was driven crazy by self-hatred. She worked, or volunteered, maybe she didn't do either, just hacked into the clinic's records. You were so close, Will. She was disgusted by the same things you found out about the girls. She killed them to purify them from their degrading lives and to make Daddy love her. He hated her for many reasons but lately because, note this fine irony, she couldn't have children. She couldn't have them because of one botched circumcision, but that wasn't going to stop her from having a second for her father. Plus she thought the second one would hide what the first had done to her. All very elaborate thinking. Except her shitty scheme was found out and ruined the multi-billion dollar alliance with the unknown groom's family. The man insulted Olivia in front of Safra. You know, Harvey said if anyone messed with Olivia, he would take it as an insult against his property. That Harvey, dead right. Olivia humiliated Safra and cost him money. She was abandoned with no hope of a family. He knew she was the killer all along. He hired me to find her with no one looking. Safra eroded my reputation and yours so no one would believe any of this. He killed her, Will. Either he or Jamal sent Olivia that bullet into her head."

Will put his elbows on his knees, clasped his hands as if he were praying. He beseeched her to be clear. "So you're not sure who killed Olivia?"

"No, I'm not. He's magic. I was there but it's like I wasn't." She put her hand in the pocket that held the ring, she was about to reveal it when they were interrupted by the sound of something hitting the front door.

Will pulled his gun, checked the peephole. When he opened the door, a large envelope fell across the threshold. It was addressed to both of them. Will put his gun on the table, then ripped the envelope open. It burst like an overripe plum, instead of a torrent of luscious nectar coming forth, a pile of blackmail cascaded in the form of photographs. Beck picked up a picture of her a bloody sock and sneaker. Will held up several shots of them with Ella, including one where they were on each side of her. She looked afraid. There was the picture of Safra holding Beck's hand in the hospital. It made him appear caring. "There's a typed note," Will reported. He read it to Beck.

"Tommy Justin was a racist and a rapist. The world is well rid of him. Olivia Safra was a victim. If there were to be another suspect or events told that are counter to Justin's complicity, then there would be a new investigation that would make certain items come to the surface including emails and texts and more. Things should be left in peace." Will stopped reading, dazed.

"That's a picture of the sock and shoe I had on last night. I bet that's Olivia's blood on them. Maybe even Tommy's?" I tried to kill myself just a few days ago, right? Isn't that what the cops say? Maybe I murdered my own client to get back at Safra. Maybe you let Tommy Justin escape to help me. Not so crazy, certainly no crazier than the truth," she said clinically

Will seethed but there was nowhere to release his anger. "No, there's a way out of this. We're going downtown, show them this, tell them fucking everything."

"Then put me in handcuffs and get a pair for you too."

Will needed something to punish, release his rage upon when the phone rang. He picked up the landline and was about to hurtle it against the wall when Katie's voice came over the answering machine. She sounded husky like people do after screaming or crying for a long period of time.

"Beck, Safra wouldn't let me be fired. Why? I did lose Focus which relegates me to cats in trees stories. Do you believe this shit about Olivia and Justin? Come the fuck on. Okay, you're not going to answer; maybe you're not there which is good. Good because Beck, oh Beck." Kate choked back sobs. "Harvey, Beck, do you know? He was killed last night, a hit and run. What the hell is going on. I'm not fired but I've been put on suspension, indefinitely. I know Will has too. It feels like the world's ending.

Janice said she would go with me; I'm getting out of here. Call me to say you and Will are joining us. We're leaving tomorrow. I'm not saying where until we've been driving for at least an hour. Pack essentials, we'll buy what we need on the road. Even if they say they got the killer, it's dangerous for us, more than ever. Call me." She hung up.

Beck couldn't cry about Harvey. The body count was too much to handle. Her sadness was too deep, too primal. She let the fury sweep over it. She let it focus her on Harvey's murder because that's what happened, cold blooded murder by Safra. The monster had a very busy night.

"He tied up all of his loose ends, didn't he?" she asked. Will looked at Beck like she was a stranger. He had finally put a horrible thought into an actual idea. "Do you realize that you and Safra were working together to find Olivia? He orchestrated it like you were a team."

The last ugly wave hit Beck, the weight of death and manipulation. She looked at Will helplessly. "Safra said pretty much exactly that. I feel like I need to be bathed in fire, purified." Will seemed to be shrinking into the sofa.

"I want to go with Kate, Beck. Let's get out of here, regroup. I have to go to the station. The so-called complaint has never been filed against me; it's a sword that they're dangling over my head to keep me in line. Until we can do something about this, we should get out of here. I have to go, it is a direct order. When I get back, be ready to leave."

Beck took Will's hand. "Will, don't forget that I am a lawyer. Please, don't answer any questions except the way they want you to and most important, don't offer them any information. No matter what happens. Promise me?"

Will tried to live a life prescribed by the poet he revered. He had strived to see things in a grand scheme and to only be limited by a limitless imagination. He thought he could dwell in a world of his own creation, instead he had been dragged into Safra's universe where he remained, imprisoned. He kissed her on the forehead and left Beck's apartment void of grand visions and flights of fancy.

Beck looked at the photographs and the note. She fingered the ring in her pocket when she suddenly remembered Miles. She had to explain things to Miles. Beck dialed the phone. "Miles? Miles, its Beck. No, the whole Justin story is bullshit. It's so much more complicated. Justin is just another one of Safra's victims. He killed Olivia. Miles, she is the one…Miles? Miles?" She dialed the phone. Miles didn't answer.

Beck drummed her fingers on what turned out to be the handle of Will's service revolver. His leaving it out of his control was a serious infraction. Leaving it with Beck was a mistake of galactic proportions.

Twenty One

Hardware stores, the domain of professional builders, handymen, and weekend craftsmen. Such stores are filled with sharp edges, blunt objects, heavy rope, toxic chemicals, and things with teeth and claws. They're really very handy for someone who can't get his hands on a gun, just get an ax. Beck trolled the aisles. She wanted to steal some relief. She held the exact same bag of bolts that ruined her life during the LeMond case. In fact, it was the exact same store, but this time something happened, or more accurately didn't happen. She didn't feel any of the comfort. There was no high. No sense of control or getting something over on another person. There was nothing except a bag of bolts in her hand and peace. It was like turning on a light, the dark was snuffed out instantly. She dropped the bag on the floor. She had no use for them. She did have a use for Will's gun.

***

City Hall was built in the style of Greek in architecture. It was an old, venerable building but in recent years the scent of graft and greed sullied its hallways. The moments where justice ruled over big money, race, and influence were becoming more and more rare. Today chaos took over all transactions. On the floor of the tundra people clamored for the arrival of Richard Safra. It was like the criminal version of waiting for the first Elvis concert. Mindless frenzy for something, but no one knew exactly what. Something always out of the ordinary occurred when Safra was in the building. The incarnation of the grieving Safra would be a perfect show for a crowd bathed in cynicism and in love with the macabre.

Beck shouldered her way to be near the microphones. From her vantage point she could see Jim not too far away. He looked bloated from false pride built on the phony ending of Tommy Justin as the killer, but there was nothing phony about complicity in Tommy's killing. The lights came on cueing the cameras where to aim like rifles in a firing squad. Beck watched Jamal in his usual subservient position ten paces behind Safra. His bandage was filthy from the charred wood of the Mosque and shoving women to their knees, and murder.

Finally, the grand entrance. Safra was draped impeccably in solid black, even the handkerchief. Who is impeccable hours after your child is found murdered? No one, unless you are the bastard who murdered the child. He was a master Kabuki artist. Believable except for his eyes; their white blue ice captured the monster within the mask.

"This is a tragic day," he began. "I thank the police department for their intrepid, dogged dedication. They put an end to my personal nightmare. The city and her people can breathe easier. For the families who lost their daughters, I grieve with you. I have told my lawyers to begin working on trusts for you and your families. Rebuilding your lives will help me rebuild my own. For the police, whom I owe so much, I have given instructions that the money that was set aside for the reward be donated to their Police Benevolent Fund. I know that there are many questions about the crimes exacted against us, but today I must be left to grieve. Excuse my brevity. I will accommodate you in the next few days. I thank you very much for coming."

Nothing, not a sound. No one challenged him. He could leave and not answer a single question about his murdered daughter. The clicks and whirs of cameras echoed throughout the vast hall. Then, like he was Elvis, a thunderous round of applause and cheers drowned out the incessant clicking of the cameras. He did a slight bow. He had conquered them. Safra left his stage. Bastard, thought, Beck, again he didn't call her Olivia or say his daughter. The thought coincided with her pulling the gun from her waistband. She knew how to get into City Hall and miss the security checks.

Safra moved to the elevators, she could get to him there. Then she heard an explosion.

Chaos built on chaos. Police plunged through the crowd. People squatted with hands over their ears, others fell flat to the ground, while others ran to where? Beck stood still. Did she fire the gun? She looked at it but was unsure. Then she saw the last straw. The horror not anticipated. Miles Gordon was wrestled to the floor. He was screaming "my baby, my baby." One cop slugged him in the head to shut him up, but he didn't. Five cops struggled to keep Miles down. As she got closer she thought of a great bull elephant being pulled down by hyenas. She got an opening when people started screaming that Safra was hit. People forgot to be afraid, or they wanted to see the wounded emperor more than they cared about their own safety. The crowd loosened up and the police were called to be in too many places.

Police radios crackled with the message to clear the hall and get the medics. Miles was being pulled up when she got close enough to scream out his name. He moved his head wildly to find her. The police tried to move him but they couldn't. Finally he caught sight of Beck. "Miles, you were supposed to wait to talk to me," she yelled.

"You said he killed my baby. What did I need to wait for? You said he killed her."

Miles was shoved past her: he saw the gun in her hand. He tried to motion for her to hide it, but the only response he got was another blow from a cop.

Beck was shocked into silence. Paralyzed but the realization that she was the reason that Miles was going to be charged. With what? Murder? Did he shoot Safra because of her? First Jasmine, now her father. Shit, why didn't she make it clearer that Olivia killed his daughter? She knew why, because she was protecting herself and Will. She had to explain this to Miles. What good would it do for him? It would do nothing for Miles, just ease her guilt. So she left him to find out when he was booked.

There was a frenzy of EMT near the elevators. The crowd moved toward the new scene of action. "What was that guy saying you told him? He just tried to kill Richard Safra because you told him something?"

Beck licked her lips. God, she was thirsty. There was no way to get Safra at that moment. Then she turned to Jim. He stood patiently for an answer to the questions he just posed. Self-satisfaction and contempt were written all over his face.

"Are you really going to pretend that you guys got the right person, Jim?"

"What I am going to act like is an arresting officer and put you in handcuffs for brandishing a firearm in a public place."

"I was just protecting myself. I heard shots. Not against the law in this county."

Jim looked at the gun carefully, an ugly smile crossed his razor thin lips. "This weapon is police issue. I bet your life that it's Blake's service revolver. This needs your presence upstairs."

Beck didn't hear him. She saw Safra being prepped to go onto a gurney. His arm and shoulder were bandaged. It could be worse than it looked. She started to walk toward him but Jim grabbed her. "You can't leave. I'm questioning you." Jim dialed his cell. "I want you to hold Blake. Yeah, he's here. If he argues, tell him I've got his girlfriend, Oldman and tell the Lieutenant I have or rather Oldman has Blake's gun. Got it? Oldman, yeah, that bitch." Beck didn't care about Jim; she only cared about getting to Safra. He grabbed her roughly, threatened handcuffs.

She turned to Jim. "The gun's a minor mix up. Let's get to the real stuff. Did you do Harvey Jim, did you? You were one of LeMond's goons. You belong to Safra too? Is that why you let an innocent man take the fall? Did you murder him?"

It was all Jim could do to not to slug the bitch. He had wanted to for a year, but she was smart and knew the law. "It's too bad you didn't shoot Safra. You might have actually killed the bastard. With one fell bullet we could've been done with you and him. You want to talk about setting people up? Are you the reason that poor bastard was taken away in cuffs? First you let his kid die, then you send him to prison. And you? Nothing will happen to you, will it? You will lawyer your way out of the gun thing, all of it. On the other hand, Blake's career is on life support. Good thing he's got a rich daddy."

It wasn't that Beck didn't hear Jim, or that she didn't agree with most of what he said, it was that she had to get to Safra.

It was impossible to get to the elevators. Then divine intervention, Jim started to move her toward Safra. She cooperated until he started to move to the stairs. She marshaled all of her strength and twisted her body free of his grasp. The medics were away from the gurney packing things and Jamal was checking the elevator car. She ran to Safra. His bandages were bloody. His face was pale and his eyes were closed. She squeezed his bandaged arm. "Too much pressure where it hurts? It's just the beginning. We're still partners." She wrenched his arm until his eyes sprung open to see her smiling.

An officer shoved her away just as Jamal was about to strike her. Beck's hand had Safra's blood on it. She held it up in Jamal's face. "You're slipping on the job. Probably tired from last night." It took three officers to pin Jamal to the wall. The medics rushed the gurney to the elevator. One convinced the police to let Jamal accompany Safra.

Jim made no attempt to intervene. He slowly made his way toward Beck. This confrontation was of interest. Why stop it? They wheeled Safra into the elevator. As the doors began to close, Beck held up her hands. One hand was covered with his blood. On the other she wore Olivia's ring. Safra motioned for Jamal to stop the doors from closing. He struggled to prop himself up. He wanted her to see that he was very much alive. It was like they were speaking. He was coming for her; she would be waiting. The doors closed.

Beck turned to Jim. "Yep," he said, "if you could've killed him, it would have tied things up, but maybe his being alive is more interesting." Beck pushed the elevator button. "I want to go upstairs and clear this gun bullshit up. Then Will and I are going away, and no one's going to touch us. And I know the charges against Miles will be dropped. You know why? Because Richard Safra will make sure they are. He will even do something about Will's situation. It makes things more interesting, just like you said. You see, he has a plan, but so do I."

Beck looked around the building that brought her a life in law. She had missed it, deeply. For the first time in a long time, she began to think she could come back, but she would have to take down a devil to do it.

About the Author

After Elizabeth S. Sullivan earned her JD while working full-time teaching English she decided to follow the advice she gave to students: follow your passion and your work will not be a job. She continued to teach, left the law behind to embrace her passion, writing. She has written five screenplays, one short, and has worked as a script doctor. She is thrilled to publish her first novel. Elizabeth has won screenplay competitions and has been a semifinalist twice, in the prestigious Nicholl competition, which garnered Elizabeth a manager in Beverly Hills. Her passions are movies, reading, politics, the environment and the two most important people in her life, Kalen and Ashley.

Made in the USA
Lexington, KY
28 November 2014